THE WAY THROUGH.

By Alex A. Wright

1.Beginnings.

Somewhere in the depths of my half-drunken teenage imagination the notion had taken hold and now refused to release me. I was sat, or rather sprawled ,at a pub table and I idly studied its surface .The scratches and indents of a thousand Saturday nights ,I reflected, were not unlike the web of roads upon a map, nor were they dissimilar to the rivers in the same landscape displayed on the same map. In the Lounge itself a song was playing. A loud old local was parodying the repetitive rhythm section and-it had to be admitted-staying in tune too as he did. I had glared at him as he did so through another, earlier number on the jukebox, even pulling a sneer, but had given up in the face of his dogged determination to mock the music that was playing and the fact that my efforts only made that determination set solid .I went instead with an option of goodwill ,got myself another drink and put one in for the old guy who so tunefully disdained alternative and rock. That had been several drinks ago-and he was still going strong. I was well into an alcoholic haze myself ,my mind going further adrift and my head resting upon the table top as the notion took hold and took me off elsewhere...

oOo

He had no time for kings ,for princes ,for parliaments and none for governments .What Trys did have was a respect for the value of learning and an acquired like for both the cold certainties of the military life and the warmer carousing it brought away from the field of battle. Upon making himself the master of this life ,he had found it was one that could also make him money-and a lot of it. He was waiting for the merchant ,who was running late, and passing the time by alternating between reading a promising book and admiring the view out across the bay. The day displayed the kind of azure blue in sea and sky that artists sometimes strive to capture: not quite otherworldly but remarkable enough to elevate the day out of the ordinary and into one to be enjoyed, one to be memorable. Across from the front of the little taverna on the bay the wooden walks glistened here and there with the wet footprints of the fishermen and their catches bulged in their nets and baskets as they brought them in to harbour. Further away ,but faintly caught upon the breeze ,the calls and other din of the town and the fish market were at the edge of his awareness.

"Do soldiers read the classics these days then? The world is indeed changing." Trys glanced up at the interruption to the little idyll he had been in whilst he waited and saw that it was the merchant. Large, beringed and glowing from the heat and too many indulgences in the way that some men will, he was almost a comic artist's image of a merchant , Trys reflected.

There was a deceptively avuncular demeanour to the man as well. Trys felt confident that it was deceptive and wasn't taken in, even for a moment. Business was business, after all- and this merchant had risen far from his roots on the streets and in the bazaar.

"I will join you, if I may, "the merchant said. Trys made a polite yet perfunctory wave with his hand ,indicating the seat opposite. Spotting an arrival ,the waiter hurried over to take the newcomer's order. As the waiter left to fetch the sugary cocktail ordered ,the merchant turned his full attention on Trys, studying him for a few seconds before he spoke again.

"My name is Osman .I represent a number of...parties...who are interested in taking advantage of the services you offer."

"Can your parties pay my fees and expenses, Mr Osman?"

"Oh yes, that won't be any problem for our little group."

"What exactly do you need then?"

"Well, as you may well be aware yourself, the overland trade routes between here and the Middle and Far East have fallen into disuse during the last few decades. We have railways now ,of course, but stubborn conflicts persist between local warlords and the outposts of the big empires which leave them...unreliable...a less than viable option as things stand for freight of value .Now war has broken out in Europe itself too and the seas are at the mercy of the warring navies. We need the old overland route free from brigands and back in business, so that we too can be back in business."

The challenge that this idea presented made Trys interested despite himself. He knew well that money could win wars but was nevertheless amused that even the war hadn't blunted Osman's appetite for commerce.

War presented its own opportunities at the same time as it had its costs, both in human misery and money ,Trys knew ,however. Despite the grim amusement taking hold of him ,he cut a laugh at Osman short .It didn't do to behave too much that way towards a prospective client.

"I shouldn't go within a mile of your assignment, "he replied," but ,well ,you've got me interested .I may be able to achieve what you need."

o0o

I was jolted awake by the sound of laughter. The landlord was looking at me with a blend of distaste and seasoned resignation.

"He's stirring now, Stan," said a female voice. Glancing groggily around ,I saw that it came from the barmaid.

 "C'mon, son," said Stan. "We close in the afternoons. Off home...or wherever...with you."

The village pub was one of those few, surely just a handful, that hadn't taken the opportunity of all day opening. I bolted for a visit to the gents before emerging dazed out into the glare of the sunlit afternoon ,all under Stan's watchful gaze. An afternoon's learning supposedly lay ahead and I checked a pocket for the key to a locker as I walked ,thoughts of retrieving my bag and books about as welcome as the growing lunchtime hangover that was stealing over my now waking self.

Oh well, it was a warm and pleasant afternoon at least. The college, one of those red-brick edifices which screamed educational establishment the moment one set eyes upon it, came into view through the trees.

I sneaked in, if I could call it that ,through the back, where students' cars ,a smoking shelter and cycle shed all lurked like wayward students from terms past ,and headed straight for the drinks machine and the chance to rehydrate.

o0o

Trys watched Osman walking away. Two individual silhouettes of minders detached themselves from the deeper shadows to join him as he left. Growing up on the streets was one thing .Leaving yourself open to their dangers ,having made good, was quite another.

Trys realised with slight surprise that he was looking forward to getting his old comrades-in-arms back together, then assembling some more fighting men as raw material to flesh out his mercenary force .If these survived, then they would find that they had quietly become quite deadly under his tutelage and now had some very...marketable...talents.

He went in search of a telegraph office. After that, he would need to find his second-in-command and prise him out of the arms of whichever unsuspecting lover he had taken up with and left under his spell. Arden had a tendency to favour pretty but intense women who were all the more appalled when they found out about his fickle nature in love and mercenary occupation.

Trys wasted no time in judging him: Arden was a damned good officer and utterly loyal to his old comrade-and they were soldiers of fortune after all. What he did away from the field of battle was his own business .It just made getting a mission underway a form of entertainment in its own right on some occasions.

The shouts and din of the fish market intensified ,as did the all-pervading marine smell of fish and seafood ,as Trys took a shortcut through it. Many avoided it but it took took quite some time off his walk -and he enjoyed its tempered mayhem anyway.

Telegrams sent ,he set out to find Arden .A little information, easily bought in this city with Osman's money, had pointed him to the Christian quarter. Arden had probably found himself a new friend there.

Trys stopped at a bookshop at the entrance to a street near the churches . He was back out and browsing some wooden tables set up outside it when a commotion broke out somewhere further down the street.

oOo

I had weathered the afternoon and was walking now to the train station for the journey home. I was listening to the conversation of two friends and watching the human tide of students that flowed in the same direction as us.

The half-acrid ,half-aromatic smell of cigarette smoke drifted through the crowd here and there .I had developed a strange kind of self-discipline that had limited my smoking to one or two on a Saturday, or a Saturday night .Financial savings aside, it left me generally more fragrant but less likely to socialise easily with the sources of smoke now floating along with us.

"I'm very English :I like tea, y' know, even with my tea-hahahah ,with my tea , geddit?"said a female voice.

"Hmmm, yeah. I used to have a mug of hot chocolate in the morning but it was making me chubby, "said her male friend.

"What, you mean FAT?"

"Well, no , y'know ,it was making me chubby. So I stopped."

"Yes but you mean it was making you fat, right?"

"No, no, chubby...a little big. Big -but not exactly fat," came the reproachful reply.

"Oh, sod off, Dave, they're the same thing!"

(We're the future . Your future ,said a mischievous thought in my head.)

With a clunk the train door closed behind me. I had lost sight of Dave and his tea-loving ,fat-hating female friend .As the old electric train lurched into life then clattered up to speed ,I watched the station and then the scenery blur. Released, my thoughts began to do the same.

Arden had appeared several minutes ago ,a severely-dressed but attractive woman at his side delivering a fluent stream of verbalised anger in quite loud Turkish .Trys had calmly and politely informed her that Arden was irredeemable and that he ,Trys, had long since ceased trying to pay off various women ,and their fathers and husbands ,for him.

The woman's expression had frozen into a blank before her hazel eyes had blazed and her knee had left Arden to dodge very quickly indeed. Eyes still aglitter, she had left them. Now the two men were in conversation, walking together down the street.

"Find out who's still in circulation. Put the word out. There's going to be a shortage of fighting men with the war on in Flanders and France...perhaps we may persuade a few away though,"Trys was saying.

"We'll need weapons. Horses, vehicles too if we can get them," Arden said.

"I believe our old cache remains intact. Our benefactor has deep pockets, or claims to. We'll have them."

Trys paused a moment.

"This suits us perfectly: both the British and the brigand in our sights."

"Trys, old friend, you *are* British, aren't you?"

"Like you, Captain Raul Arden ,I am a man of the world."

It was just one brief mention of a military title but it seemed in an instant to bring the two of them back to a place, a working relationship ,left off at some point in the past. An air of understanding and a kind of mutual respect also became evident in that same moment. Finding a taverna, they were soon talking whilst scrawling written plans on scrounged paper. When they parted, they parted each with his tasks assigned for setting up their campaign.

Trys could later be seen sat ,once again, on the waterfront ,so deep in thought as to seem almost in a trance by the lamplit water's edge. As he made off to where he was lodging, two figures watched from a high window above the street.

"Is he one of ours, brother?" asked one.

"No ,no, he is solitary where our arts are concerned."

"Solitary? I thought we had put an end to all that sort of thing..."

"Our current head has...something like tolerance...where these renegades are involved."

"He cannot mind, surely ,if two of his loyal brothers were to watch one such renegade, just to see that nothing that would be unfortunate for our brotherhood went unnoticed."

oOo

My key opened the back door with a little jiggling and some familiar metallic meddling sounds and then I was inside and home. The kettle went straight on, filled from the noisy tap. As it made its way to a boil, I deposited my bag upstairs ,returning to brew a welcome tea..

I took the tea in its lightly steaming mug with me to the semi-sanctuary of my bedroom and after selecting something to listen to on the stereo, I threw myself onto my bed and got stuck in to writing an adventure for later in the week.

The maps of a wizard's island fortress were coming together well. A few finishing touches and it would be time to fill the place with the life of a narrative and the pitfalls of traps, adversaries and monsters.

Of course ,homework and coursework should have come first .It really should have-but it didn't give me an escape in the same way that creating an adventure in a campaign did.

The contemporary mysticism of the goth music filling my bedroom suited the overall mood of my afternoon pastime :guitars wreathed in effects, fleeting flashes of eerie synths, all driven by a drum machine and sung over in deep tones ,it gave rise to a sort of gloomy, psychedelic and esoteric atmosphere.

it also sounded damned good, as far as I was concerned. Neighbours' opinions had been known to differ...

oOo

The dagger thudded, juddering, into the doorframe. Unfazed, Arden plucked it free, threw it whence it came. He heard it clatter, useless, off a wall. Soft footsteps fled away .The faintest hint of a shadowy shape went with them. He hurled his empty glass after the shape in a moment's frustration.

"You appear to have attracted someone's interest, Arden. This could prove entertaining, provided it doesn't hinder our endeavour too much."

Try's face became, briefly, almost completely expressionless and his eyes very nearly vacant. After a few seconds, expression returned and he began to laugh quietly.

14

"I have half an idea that your would-be assassin was female ,"he said.

"Oh well...so now I will need to check women for knives before we enjoy each other's company ,"Arden replied.

"You could ,of course, simply refrain from enjoying their company for a while...."

A look of mock horror took hold of Arden's face.

"Trys, what kind of monster has being idle made you, that you suggest such a thing?"

"One that wants your mind on our mission and you alive to help carry it out, perhaps."

A handful of those recruits already assembled were inside at the bar and busy bonding over a drink of something disreputable produced locally. Arden was due to travel to France that afternoon to gather more men. Trys would continue to do the same here.

Trys spoke again.

"We've got three of the new Vickers guns on the way .That should help to make us a very deadly nuisance indeed .Those can go in carriages to keep 'em mobile .I'll look at a couple of heavier guns but we will have a better edge by being mobile and agile ,so that's what I want us to be. That way lies the future of warfare, my friend, mark my words...not being stuck in a ditch ,shivering, and waiting to be a crow's breakfast."

"I'm not ready to be dead. I'm very much ready to be richer though, "said Arden.

"I'm meeting some Russians later who feel the same way .If what their spokesman told me is true, they'll be most useful to us. They grew tired of being hungry but they're excellent fighters and still hungry now -but for action and a way out of the growing chaos at home."

Two men flew, in a blur ,from the tavern door, hitting the cobbles. They landed ,still trading blows.

"Ours?"Trys asked.

Arden confirmed this with a nod. Trys stalked forward. One of the men had the advantage. An arm came back to punch. The arm shot forward .Trys grabbed it ,twisted it, then sent the man flying ,to land ,sprawling ,across the street .The second man blinked, surprised, before his face hardened. Both sprang at Trys, one snarling. Trys calmly kicked one mans legs from under him. An elbow to the other's neck left him winded ,and upended too. Before either could recover, Trys took each in turn, throwing them roughly ,at the wall.

He drew a breath and waited. The two groaned and began to pull themselves up. They did not try to go for him again ,however.

"Gentlemen ,whilst I am paying you, I am in charge of you .I am not, however, some simpering dandy. Should you cross me again ,it will be your last mistake. Understood?"

The two straightened and said yessirs. A few minutes later they were back in the loudness of the bar.

o0o

"I don't believe it…he never even tasted…"

My little circle of role-gaming friends were looking at me in amazement and I did not quite understand why-yet. Something like a collision between comprehension and foreboding was creeping into my consciousness now though.

"Tasted what, Pete?"

"Tasted two whole teaspoons of soy sauce in your tea, is what."

"What the hell did you do that for?!"

Though skinny, spotty and generally blotchy ,Pete was utterly unfazed by his own appearance. He was equally unperturbed by my annoyance.

"We've been looking for a chance to get you back for putting almond flavouring round the coffee cups after you read about cyanide smelling a bit like almonds in that spy novel. Guess we're quits now."

I briefly considered destroying their entire adventuring group in the game later on but I realised that that would be petty revenge- and less likely to make me a Games Master they'd respect than taking it all in my stride might.

"Bastards, "I said with a rueful smile.

Five infernal minutes of being told how and why I had deserved it followed. Eve, Pete, Myron, Rich and I then moved on ,back to our game.

"Rich, put some more music on. Let's get back to this campaign."

He began rummaging amongst the CDs on the side and soon the sounds of heavy rock filled the electric-lit space of the small and, consequently, crowded bedroom.

"So, you've come across a group of orcs..."I reminded them.

"If I say 'We say sorry and wipe it off ,' will you blow up my character?"

"Almost certainly."

"What are the orcs doing?"

"Drawing swords and nocking arrows, mostly."

"Okay. Can we roll for initiative, please, G.M.? If we get it,I have just the spell for this in my new spell book..."

"Roll."

oOo

Whilst Osman hadn't much enjoyed paying out more money for expenses during Trys' visit ,he had been more enthusiastic in receiving news of the progress in assembling the small fighting force. The Russians had now become the latest additions ,their spokesman accepting the wages offered and relayed to his countrymen that whilst Trys paid ,they obeyed. Some were clearly the educated sons of wealthy families ,if hardened a little by their time as officers in a war of growing horror, but none of them were keen to return home to a country full of upheaval.

Finding a new battle to fight would help them to feel they were not cowards for that-and the pay would help to fill their bellies again. Trys knew that Russians viewed weakness and cowardice with more distaste than most...and well ,all men had to eat .If they could shoot straight, march hard and follow orders, then it was all the same to him otherwise.

Soon ,they would all be on a journey to give the British Empire a headache wherever they could and give Osman's business partners and allies as much opportunity as possible to get their goods through. A viable way using the old silk roads was the ideal outcome...a staggering challenge for such a small band of mercenary soldiers, but one which he had accepted and planned to meet. Word had come from Arden, via telegram, that he would return in four days with more men-enough men to complete their little army. Another half dozen men had also been drawn to join them here in the city, most of them hardened fighters and shrewd survivors.

Out of sight of Trys but well aware of his presence ,a woman who called herself Avçi was busy cleaning her weapons .A set of vicious-looking throwing knives were set out on a cloth and a bolt-action rifle lay to one side. Her eyes narrowed to small, gleaming shards within the shadows as she went over her plans in her mind ,all the while still cleaning and sharpening with her hands. Her instructions had been clear enough. Cause disruption. Cause alarm if possible. Kill only when the order was given. Avçi could be patient. Her time would come.

Back in the broad daylight of the busy square , Trys was forming plans of his own plans formed of a mix of military tactics and sheer brigandry. The air there was filled with the noise and stink of the day in the city; the shouts of people, the clatter of cartwheels on the stones of the square and streets...the sounds of thousands of people living in close proximity. Trys' mind, meanwhile, was off elsewhere-on matters of warfare and death in places far from there. The day drew on.

oOo

My mind fizzed with the strange feeling of both excitement and weariness I always had at the end of a campaign adventure ,as I closed the front door and said good night to them all. Turning to take the stairs to my room ,I knew sleep would be some way off yet. The stairs made their faint and familiar creaking complaint as I ascended.

In my room ,I loaded a cassette into my Walkman. The click of its closing and the whirr as it began to play the tape were unusually loud in the otherwise silent late night setting. I undressed as I listened-a knack I had developed. I took gratefully enough to my bed but picked up a book anyway to help occupy my mind until it stilled.

An hour later I was still awake. First listening carefully for the sound of either parent being awake ,I took a can of lager from its hiding place. Pulling the ring ,I swallowed a few unhelpfully warm mouthfuls before sitting the red and green vessel on the bedside table and going back to my music and reading. Periodical swigs as I read seemed to do the trick and before too long sleep finally took hold of me and drew me into it depths.

I awoke somewhere within that dead and abandoned time of night that is around three a.m., to find the house utterly still, its silence as pervasive in its way as the noise we had made the previous evening. It was a lonely time of night too ,for seldom was there another person to be found awake-and I would not exactly have been thanked for waking anyone!

Plugging headphones into my main stereo, I set a record playing and let the music fill my mind, to take it away from the stillness and nothingness of a time so early in the morning that it was still considered night. I think I must have awoken just once more before the light of day came in, for I had flipped the LP over at some point to play the other side.

I could hear the noise of a later and more populated time of day now in the distance through the window-left ajar the night before :schoolchildren calling noisily to one another-a few years ago that was me-as they made their way in, traffic and the argument of car horns that punctuated the rush hour. Noise that meant I was late! Swearing an oath fit for one of my gaming characters, I flew out of bed and threw myself together for college.

oOo

"You have done well, old friend. Wherever did you find this disreputable bunch?"

Trys was looking over the men with which Arden had returned from France ,Flanders and thereabouts. Arden, meanwhile ,was busily making acquaintance with lunch .He paused mid-chew.

"Where we agreed I would look .One or two from places further away .All of them will fight,of course."

"Hmm. Well, they´re clearly all bastards, they´ll be perfect! Have you had any more encounters with your little friend?"

"No. The only thing that nearly had me was a bottle of bad wine .I was spoilt by growing up on good Spanish red ,I guess, "he added ruefully.

The supplies and arms would be ready by the end of the week-both their mothballed things and those bought with Osman's money. Now he had to decide the route on which to take these mismatched but capable combatants to the field. It would be either Suez or overland. He had a few days to decide but he could better use these on organising the rest of logistics. He would ask Arden and get his opinion. The man *was* in some ways irredeemable but his instincts, if it was instincts that did it ,on such matters were seldom wrong.

"Land or sea ,Captain Arden...what do you think?"

"Sea. It's simple, Colonel :in this corner of the world we are nicely tucked away in the land of the Ottoman and miles from the front. We can risk it and it will be quicker."

Trys knew a ship's captain who would nicely fit the bill. There was half a chance he might even be in port here at present.

"I am going down to the waterfront to see if I can track down a certain Captain Maguire. It should be simple enough if he's in port ,"said Trys.

"Shall I show these sorry dogs how to shoot straight while you're gone?"

"Yes, good idea .Make a day of it...I will see you at the Tavern tonight."

Mark Maguire was indeed easy enough to find, supervising his crew at cleaning and repairs whilst himself working on bits of a bulky and primitive marine radio. A big man ,he was tall ,broad-shouldered and thick-limbed ,and yet there was also a glint of guile and quick wit in his eyes.

His ship was as anachronistic as she was impressive. An old tea clipper, built to carry tons of precious tea fast to a thirsty British Isles, her imposing hull and towering masts dwarfed many of the other vessels around. Few like her had been on the water, however ,for decades and decades. Trys had a feeling she had simply gone missing when the clipper fleets went to be scrapped. He wasn't ever about to ask if that feeling was correct, however.

Maguire studied Trys briefly.

"They told me you were dead. You've made quite the recovery ,"he told him.

"Good morning Mark. How's it going? Business good?"

"I can't complain. There's a war on. There's plenty of work so long as I don't get sunk."

"How would you feel about a voyage down the Suez Canal?"

"Would it make me richer?"

"It would."

"Then I would most probably feel like taking it," said Maguire." When are you travelling?"

"We'll be ready to go within a week now."

"Right...well, I better let this lot ashore for some leave then. Don't need a mutiny on my hands. I have a drop of something in my cabin for myself. If you'd care to join me, we can discuss our little voyage further."

"It's a bit early....but yes, thank you, why not?"

As he led the way below, Maguire glanced back before saying, "She still asks me every time I go back home...Have I seen you, have I heard news of you, you know."

For a moment ,a moment gone as quickly as it came, there was a fleeting, almost imperceptible break in Trys' usual impenetrable demeanour.

"You know yourself-and know better than most-what happened there."

"Aye, that I do. Well, don't get us sunk on this expedition of yours then and I'll have no further cause to think less of you."

Several hours' wrangling and a significant amount of Irish whiskey later, something like a bargain on a passage by sea had been struck. Trys sat down slightly more heavily than usual at the tavern table on his return. This was the only sign he let slip that he had just had a skinful. Arden looked across at him with a look made of both enquiry and amusement.

"Your sea captain friend still drinks like one of the fish then, it seems ,"said Arden ,"and you with him today."

"It will be worth the headache later. Our ship is secured. How was the shooting, anyway?"

"I've seen far worse. By the end of the day, it was almost like I'd never seen better. Almost. One idiot got distracted and score a six foot grouping, shooting his friend's target."

"Keep an eye. If it happens again, pay him off and pack him off. We have too much money to be made here to afford silly mistakes being made."

"Yes, sir."

"I'm going to get some rest .I need it. Our friend could drink the legendary Hercules under the table. As it stands, we sail this weekend. Tomorrow ,I had better update our patron."

Three people watched Trys and Arden go to their lodgings .Two lost interest quite quickly when Trys did nothing more spectacular than make his way back without staggering .The third threw a dagger .It flew, striking a rainwater butt. It stopped ,thrumming .Right next to Arden's head .Arden and Trys whirled round. The street was already empty, however.

Arden went to throw this one back too. Trys stopped him.

"Keep it. Perhaps we will get to return it eventually. Personally."

Arden grunted ,but stuck the blade in his belt anyway ,and they continued on their way. Through the spaces between the black silhouettes of the buildings ,all along the street, starlight and a half moon gave a fair amount of illumination .An occasional lantern ,a grudging concession to the concept of streetlighting, added to it.

Moments before they reached Trys' lodging, they heard a familiar sound :a rifle bolt being cocked A shot split the silence, missing Arden by millimetres ,shattering a lantern. Arden swore. Trys span round. Three shots rang out in reply .As the shroud of night threw its quiet once more over the scene, Trys lowered his revolver with a remarkably steady hand and indicated that Arden should join him inside. The silence in the street was sudden and a stark contrast to the noise moments earlier .Away on a nearby rooftop, Avci smiled quietly to herself ,happy that her current masters would be pleased enough with her night's work.

"I doubt our friend out there intended to hit one of us ,"said Trys once they were out of the street and in the relative safety of his lodgings," no, someone wanted to send us a simple message...well, since Dublin, profit has been my only motive in soldiering ,what it can make for us and our men. This gives us cause to ask for a higher fee and pay the men better as a result...or refuse the assignment altogether. For enough, we can be deaf to the simple message...and what happens there can be Osman's worry, not ours."

"Trys, these were scare tactics from some amateur sniper...to hell with them!"

Trys laughed.

"Oh, I agree ,my friend....but business is business....and this puts up our price."

o0o

Standing on the station ,I lit a cigarette and waited whilst the nicotine hit and helped me –to my mind-to wake up .I was also busily draining a can of cola in place of my morning tea. The train drew in with its mournful electric wail and I waited for it to stop altogether.

Once aboard ,I stuck a cassette into the Walkman an slammed it shut as firmly as I just had done with the train door. I hit play and the whirr of the mechanism and fizzing in the headphones gave way to music.

The train took off in its ever-more-rapid clatter along the tracks toward college. I watched the town recede through the window and tried to wake up and to think about the day ahead. Arriving ,I joined the tide of student humanity flooding into the village .At one point we sufficient in number to stop the traffic just by crossing the road in volume.(Pedestrian power ,hahahaha!)

One angry driver lost patience and-with much noise and a rubber-torturing, smoking wheelspin-forced his van through the flow to mock applause ,cheers and jeers. At the small patch of dirt and tree stumps that passed as a

29

smoking area(just) I struck up a conversation with a couple of the more yuppie people I knew and who, perhaps unsurprisingly, entertained talking to me because I'd gone to an independent secondary school .The materialistic subject matter of our chat left me feeling empty and unsatisfied though and I made my excuses and left for Geography class.

Finding myself to be several minutes early and finding the classroom empty,I got my stuff out and lowered my head gratefully onto my arms for a rest.

o0o

The following morning found Arden back amongst the men, training them and helping to perfect their existing skills wherever he could. Somewhere in the middle of the morning ,he was having an acceptable cup of coffee with the tavern owner. The man was an old friend ,or the closest that a soldier of fortune had to one at least.

"Raul...Señor Arden...your men who stay here...they all ask me why the Colonel hates his own country so much .I have no answer because I do not know."

"Ohh... hate? No, no, my friend, it was not hate that made Trys leave England and the army behind. He had a very cosy little post at Dublin Castle and an Irish sweetheart...but the girl's father wouldn't accept an Englishman...*any* Englishman...for his daughter. That's all I know myself, really...but he resigned his commission and left Ireland. He hasn't been back there ,or back to England

30

,for a few years now. So no....it was not hate, exactly ,that did it..."

"Captain Arden, are you being indiscreet simply to get a cup of coffee out of our friend here?"

Trys had appeared almost as though he had materialised out of thin air, right in front of them .It was the man himself though ,and not an apparition .Arden gave a start ,nearly spilling his coffee.

"One day ,sir, you must teach me that trick, "he said.

"Hmm .Perhaps .Well ,I have secured a very grudging increase in our fee. I think we need to let our current employer see that his money will be well spent now. Maguire will be good to set sail as scheduled. Soon we will be back in the field again ,old friend."

"Better than staying round these streets. I'm looking forward to it."

"Anything for you ,sir?" asked the landlord.

"Yes .I'll try this coffee of yours, which my comrade here clearly rates so highly. Thank you."

The coffee served, the tavern keeper withdrew himself. Gossip and small talk could glean valuable ,even profitable, information sometimes but regular customers were a surer source of income. The aroma of the coffee, simultaneously acrid and pleasant, permeated the space.

"Do we have any outstanding shots in this batch of recruits, Captain?"

"Two, no more...the rest are good enough...now...but nothing exceptional."

"Two will have to do, then. We have me as well."

It was a statement of fact, nothing more. There was no arrogance behind it. Arden made a rueful face. Trys viewed Arden as the best second-in-command he knew. Both of them would die to save the other, if ever it came to it. However ,he viewed Arden as simply a good shot and nothing exceptional. That said, Arden wasn't a man to upset if he had a knife to throw ,or throw back.

Trys continued:

"I've been reading some accounts from the American Civil War and the Boer War .I have a few little ideas about how we can use our marksmen .We're mercenaries ,Raul, so honour be damned! Tell our two sharpshooters there is extra money for every enemy officer of the rank of Captain or above killed-killed and confirmed killed ,of course."

"I'll set up two of the Lee-Enfields specially then for the...competition ,"said Arden.

"Good...now let's round up this rabble and share the good news with them."

oOo

"…..Wakey , wakey!!We don't want to sleep through the *whole* lecture, now do we?"

I groggily opened my eyes and then woke up ,fully ,with a start. The classroom was now very much occupied and the lecture was in full swing.

"Someone should've had a coffee before class ,Mr Tegan hahahahah!" said one of my classmates in a display of un-solidarity.

Mr Tegan turned his bespectacled face back to the whiteboard without further comment .He was capable of being almost kind at times. At times.

"Exploitation versus Development in the Brazilian Rainforest ,people."

"More coffee plantations ,pahahaha!" came a wisecrack from somewhere near the back.

Tegan could be almost kind. Others just never knew when to stop. College could occasionally be much like school. The lecture ground on before eventually coming to its end .I waited for the space to empty and then after a few moments I left as well. Taking refuge in a corner of the library, I wrote up my few notes from the lecture before going on to do some writing of my own.

After a while ,I paused and looked around. Sunlight slanted in beams through the windows, ,splashing patches of brighter colour here and there. The people here in the hushed room were a mixed bag; some seriously studying, others just killing time on a free period and others still bookishly reading novels .The middle category probably won it on numbers ,though .I went back to writing.

Some time later ,and smiling in delayed amusement at the comments in the lecture earlier ,I went in search of coffee. The college canteen stuff wasn't up to much. It was worth getting glared at by the girl in the café for the quality of the coffee. The glare said that students were the source of all ills...or certainly that she felt we were the source of all her own.

Under the glare ,I took my coffee to a window table and sat myself down .Two other students walked past outside and one gurned a face in at me before they both burst out laughing. I just laughed back-a trick I had finally learned. It seemed to mostly work .Only once had I been offered violence for it but the person failed to make good on their offer anyway .More often ,it diffused the situation in some way.

I watched some more of student-kind saunter ,stalk, or shuffle by .A few broke into a run ,late for a bus or train. Shortly afterwards ,I could hear the semi-distant sound of a train upon the tracks, coming into the village station. I made my way back down to college and and the next lecture. Later, as I sat on the rattling train ,I realised I had weathered the day quite well after a false start.

oOo

2.Following

"Thank God you never joined the Navy, son," said Maguire.

"What does he say? "asked the Russian.

"He says one thing....he means another thing," explained Arden ,"he means that if you were sailor, his crew would have thrown you overboard by now."

The Russian's face remained a perfect mask of incomprehension for a few seconds before he erupted into laughter and ,clapping Maguire hard on the back, said:

"You funny man, Mr Captain, sir, funny man!"

"That's me son, a laugh every golden minute. Please try not to piss my crew off again though."

Resentment had eventually built up in the hard-working but easy-going crew at the Russian's imperious attitude towards some of them. Whilst he had meant no malice, his view that he was one of a group of paying passengers and should be treated well accordingly was logical and normal to him but did not sit well with the mariners. Charm, cajoling and a few threats ,washed down with a draught of humour and some diplomacy, had cured the crisis. Trys and Maguire worked well together on such occasions.

Trys had since disappeared below decks and was installed in the Captain's cabin, reading and reflecting. Later he would be back above ,visible and vigilant as the mission approached .A leader should be seen by his men, and often ,Trys knew and in a way belong to them too.

In Maguire's cabin there was little light right now, enough only to illuminate the pages of the heavy books Trys was reading. From time to time he marked a page or an item, or murmured a few words to himself, sometimes writing in a neat hand, before closing his eyes and seeming to rest or medidate for several minutes.

Swimming gracefully and naturally, Avci took just moments to reach the small fishing vessel again. Ignoring the ribald comments from his two crew, she allowed the captain to help her aboard,

"Hey, little fish, would you like to come for a moonlight swim hahahahahah?"said one.

"There is something in your boot," she replied in almost bored tones.

"What?Wh-"

Glancing down, sputtering and rapidly reddening, he saw the vicious- looking gleam of a throwing blade in his left boot. It had pierced the leather but missed his toes .He had missed its flight altogether.

The captain laughed quietly.

"She has spirit, boys. She'd have you both for breakfast too!"

"Please keep the cutter just in sight on the horizon from now on, Captain. It's a risk we run ,of losing her ,but it must be done. Just within visibility ,ok?"

"Yes, my dear ,as you wish. You're paying....or someone is."

"Thank you, sweetie ,"she replied with a flawlessly sarcastic smile.

Later, when Avci was busying herself with something in the tiny cabin, the captain spoke to the crew.

"If one of you upsets her again, he's swimming home. She may be a bitch but her money is good, ok? If she starts to look like too much of a liability, maybe we'll think again ,all right ,but for now...she gets treated like she's the Caliph's daughter."

The two muttered darkly and turned away to manage the sails.

"...said, no your grace, I cannot have been it ,in the company of your sister in the manner you suggest, because I can still play a guitar, "finished Arden.

Maguire laughed heartily. Arden passed him the wine. The two had left the first mate in charge and were busy with a half-decent bottle of red that Arden had found somewhere undisclosed. A shadow fell across them but didn't disperse their good mood altogether. Trys had emerged onto the top deck.

"Is he *still* expanding that anecdote, Mark?"

Maguire regarded him with eyes shrewd despite the wine.

"Oh ,I like a nice story ,who doesn't now, even if that's all it is. He knows your own ,of course. Well, colonel, we've taken the afternoon off. Care to join us?"

The first mate cast a wistful glance toward the three ,made somehow more comical by the fact it came from a scarred and sea-hardened face, before going back to the delegated task of command. The breeze was enough to fill the sails and keep the old clipper gliding through the waves and across the azure surface of the sea. The sun smiled on the scene, seeming happy to grace such bonhomie.

More bottles were polished off between the three and the sun was long set by the time they turned in. Some of the men had joined them in the early evening and things had grown jovial indeed before the party broke up for the night.

o0o

The gothic girl was pretty and made all the more striking still by the all black eyeliner and silver jewelley she wore. She was listening in an absent ,half-distracted sort of way to Yorkie whilst looking over at the bodies dancing badly out on the dancefloor .They were silhouettes ,variously lurching, gyrating, headbanging and making strange arm movements under coloured lights shone through rather a lot of dry ice.

"You're speeding, aren't you, you little shit?" she suddenly asked him, standing up and peeling away ,fast, for the dancefloor.

Yorkie's face dropped, albeit briefly, before he bemoaned having just told her his life story for only to get that result and launched straight into another amphetamine-driven anecdote. I seemed to have landed the job of keeping him company on his latest outing, or at least this stage of it .All our other friends, and now the gothic too, had , strangely, dispersed.

Yorkie launched into a story about his journey south.at that point I made a decision I nodded towards the dancefloor, headed off and hoped he either joined me there or found another audience. I felt a little guilty about my my friend, but it had already been four hours .I felt I'd already been fairly patient .(Later,I discovered he had, indeed, found an audience and gone home with them-which let me feel vindicated too.)

I moved back to the benches from the floor. As I sat down, I spotted two friends from college and sprang back up to go and say hello. The effort to be sociable paid off by way of a lift home with their folks. As the sun snuck under and also around the edges of my curtains later that morning, I woke very briefly before going back off. Not a bad night out that, I drowsily thought.

oOo

The rain danced in countless splashes on the surface of the sea, making pockmarks in the waves beneath him .Beyond the glow of the ship's lanterns the night hid nearly everything. The sailor struggled to relight his pipe but finally won the battle there and turned back to his tour of the deck and his watch.

Close to where the clipper and the waves met, a figure sprang away backwards ,before diving almost noiselessly beneath the waves ,to emerge well beyond the lanterns' light. A small charge, not enough to sink the ship but enough to cause some headaches, some alarm and some work, would shortly go off.

Avci surfaced into the rain and looked back briefly before continuing her swim back to the small fishing boat.

"Get those fires out! Hold her steady...as she goes .Less sail, less, less. Soon as she slows to a near stop ,drop the anchor..."

Maguire was absolutely furious but simultaneously in his element, fighting the odds, the sea and a stricken ship.

The sailor who doubled-up as ship's carpenter hurried over to tell him:"I can have her patched up in an hour or two .I can do a little more by daylight. The rest is gonna have to wait till we can put into port...but short of something like this happening again ,or a typhoon ,she'll be fine."

"Do it! Mine ,was it, Ochintyre?"

No, Cap ,this was set by hand ,is my guess ,and by a clever saboteur. A mine would have sent us to the bottom. They knew exactly how to hole her but not sink her .Bastards!"

"Thanks, man. Sorry for the extra work."

"You're fine .Beats building coffins like I usually get to do."

This set Maguire laughing quietly but helplessly to himself for a few moments. The decks were a lantern-lit scene of well-organised but but rapid action ,the combination of lanterns and a few primitive electric lights giving it all an eerie feel, something almost ethereal.

Trys walked up. He had sent some of his own men to assist, partly as it made sense, since they all wanted to stay afloat and partly because he saw it as a chance to defuse any more potential animosity.

"Raul and I have had a discussion. We're going to cut you in. You asked me not to get you sunk, after all."

Which had Maguire laughing softly again.

"You've not managed that just yet, my friend. But fine ,the extra money will help the crew to have short memories about this."

Avci looked out from her vantage point and across the glittering waters. The sun sparkled its light playfully on the ripples of the waves and the air was warm. Maguire had anchored just long enough to put the private army ashore. Once his men had finished, the rowing boats had been hauled up and stowed on board swiftly and the wounded old clipper had set sail.

It would, Avci felt, have been a shame to have sent such a fine vessel to the bottom. There was something rather majestic about her ,a sense of freedom to her ,that struck a chord with the young assassin.

Shaking her head sharply to dispel her reflections-she was working ,she couldn't afford to get sentimental right now-she checked her rifle and blades before rolling away from the clifftop and the skyline. She then stood and made off at a slight crouch. She would be waiting ,contemplating her next move as Trys' force headed inland.

"Raul, do you still have our little friend's knife?"

"You already know it, Trys."

"Ok, let's have it then please, Captain."

Arden sighed before rummaging in his tunic and digging out the throwing dagger to pass across.

"May this not involve your little hobby ,"Arden said.

"It involves trying to help our cause, old friend. You don't need to know any more than that."

That evening ,as the men sat around swapping ever more exaggerated stories, ones that grew with embellishments added in each subsequent telling ,like soldiers sometimes do, Trys moved away from the circles of light around the small campfires and walked quietly away to the tent to the tent put up solely for his use. He stepped in and stepped out of the noises and outside the campfires.

As the men drifted off much later to their blankets, and perhaps to the land of dreams , Trys emerged and sat quietly sipping some tea he had just made. The sentries saw him but said nothing. Following orders paid well. Asking too many questions did not.

After the sun had made a some of its journey towards noon, the skies grew full of the promise of rain once again and clouds obscured the sunlight. Arden and two of the men went to the small bazaar in the nearby walled town, to top up supplies and buy information .They had some success with both things, and it was almost dusk as they left the walls.

A light rain started and became steadily heavier until it was a downpour .Two shots rang out, the only other sound ,except the rain, close together. Two cracks sounded too. Right next to Arden .A saddlebag sprung holes. Sprung two streams of dried beans .

Arden swore .The animal, however, did not start, did not bolt.

Thankful for the steady nerves of the warhorse, he turned and looked back. The visibility was poor in the rain and retreating light. He and the two men chose to head back and save dying for another day.

Behind the walls, Avci's world was suddenly one of pain .From nowhere came sharp flashes of pain. They went through her, had her doubled over. They would clear briefly, but come back seconds later. Only her pride kept her from writhing and moaning with the agony of it. Through gritted teeth she still managed to hiss;

"Bastard…..you will pay for this….bastard….."

Some few minutes later, she pulled herself together and moved away from her hiding place by the town wall. Donning her disguise anew, she drifted in a dazed fashion ,through streets slowly muddying under the rain ,towards the town gate.

"Hurry, woman!We lock the gate in 15 minutes! I don't want your dad or your old man on my case!"

The disguise had done its work: the fool guard clearly took her for a farm girl from the surrounding countryside. She hid her contempt and played along. Her impression of a local peasant girl was frighteningly convincing, and her Persian was more than passable.

"Sorry ,sir, sorry…"

"Get off home with you! There has already been shooting….I don't need any more trouble tonight!"

She could sense the guard watching her from the gate as she headed up the highway then onto a narrow farm trail. The world was still run by men, and, whatever the guard had said, well, most of them still thought with their privates, she concluded. No matter…she got a kick out of swimming against the current, and whilst what had happened to her at the wall had unsettled her much more

than she liked, she was rallying fast .She changed route a
little and went in search of advice.

Incredibly, I found a girlfriend that summer-
or,possibly,she found me.Going to the same small seaside
town every year for holidays had meant that I half knew a
few of the local kids.The annual trip finally had an extra
benefit.One of the locals and I suddenly saw each other
through the prism of adolescence and started to see a lot
of each other that fortnight.Her taste in music was dire
but we could work on that and,in fairness,she felt the
same about mine.

"Wham?!Are you actually serious?"

"We can't listen to your stuff...it's like being at a funeral!"

Feeling myself drawn into the depths of her brown eyes,I
decided to let my reply slide.

Some hours later, we were walking back to the caravan
park after a night out ,with her friend in tow. Behind us
on the narrow country lane, somewhere further down the
snaking length of dark hedgerows, music, the sound of an
engine and two darting headlight beams-seen

occasionally as the vehicle took a corner-were approaching quite fast to invade the moment.

"That's Just The Way It Is," by Bruce Hornsby And The Range, was playing extremely loudly as the car came close, very much audible through the the open driver's window. Oh no....I knew whose anthem that was this summer-and they knew me.What were the chances,all the way out here?

The car stopped and slowed, and the driver's window was lowered further .It was .It was Glen Jones.

"All right ,mate? Who's the gooseberry, then?"

Without waiting for a reply ,he put the window back to half open and drove off. The metallic blue XR3i was soon gone from sight and hearing, possibly leaving me with a small diplomatic incident to defuse. Then again, possibly not: my girlfriend had just broken into gales of laughter.

"Poor Jonno..."followed by more laughter.

Jonno began to smile ,then laugh a little too. That could have gone a lot worse, I decided. Ten minutes later, I was back in our caravan.Some time after that I was alone again and and asleep. The following morning I got up early and went for a walk along the pebble beach.

The pale blue of the sea was almost as still as a millpond. There was just the slightest hint of a breaking wave at the very water's edge, which broke with the gentlest of splashes and a small sigh over the stones. The sun was less than an hour into the sky and lent a sparkle to the waves in a sky also blue but faintly tinged pink with the last vestiges of a fading night-time mist.

It was Saturday morning. I lit a cigarette ,the flavour pungent and almost alien in the clear morning air as I took the first drag on it.I carried on walking ,my footsteps crunching along the stony beach as I went. Five minutes later I arrived at the seafront café and took a seat outside ,waiting for it to open. Ten minutes later I was sat in front of a pot of tea and waiting for a sizeable breakfast of pancakes and syrup ,an American import as breakfasts went .If I was fortunate, my girlfriend would stick her head in at the café to say hello before she went on to her part-time job.

There she was, looking better after a late night than I thought possible, at least if my own appearance earlier was anything to go by .A little lurch of excitement gave me momentary butterflies somewhere in the middle of my chest. She walked over, with her heels clicking and fashionably big hair perfectly styled .I gazed admiringly at her as she approached. She smiled a little as she noticed. Life, I concluded ,could be good.

oOo

Stupid….stupid…how could she have *been* so stupid? Of course! It was so obvious…. So easy. Simply don't believe it and it will fail to work on you. You must hold firm to your indifference, your disbelief in the working of spells but if you do that it will fail. That was what the old Imam had said. Well, what had said once he understood that he wasn't off to meet the Almighty just yet but rather, that he would ,in fact, be well-remunerated for his advice. The missionary Catholic priest had said much the same, with advice to trust in the Lord and only Him, when she had used her mother's teaching and her childhood catechesis to sound him out.

As with all her targets, she took time to get to know their habits and their backgrounds, their beliefs and interests. Things had been quiet for a month or two before this work and ,keen to get back into an assignment, she had become so absorbed in studying Trys and Arden that she had let it cloud her usual judgement and self-control. It wasn't going to happen again.

She had a clear shot ,though over distance, on Trys right now. If she killed him, that was contrary to her instructions. She looked briefly at his second-in-command, noticed something, dismissed it for now and put it away for future consideration. Regulating her breathing, she checked the range on the sight and let herself relax slightly. Smiling almost imperceptibly, she held her aim and applied steadily-increasing pressure to the trigger.

The pin struck the round. The shot sounded, loud. Arden spun around but it was Trys who had fallen down ,clutching a leg. The Captain crossed himself and squatted down to help his friend. She couldn't see expressions or very small things from here but she could imagine the rest of the scene in perfect detail. She clutched her rifle to her, rolled away, stood and ,shouldering it, walked calmly away through the trees.

Later, in the camp, Raul Arden was whispering Ave Marias to himself when the doctor approached.

"The Colonel will recover. He is very fit for man his age. Some rest and keep all clean."

"Thank you. And never have told us there was a doctor hidden in your number….we could have paid you better."

"What would I do with it Captain ?My wife and child were murdered by Bolsheviks…now I live to forget and try to forgive .I can't…but I try."

Arden smiled and clapped the man on the shoulder.

"Well, I thank you anyway. I am sure of that the Colonel has too. May you have a good rest."

"Thank you. And you. Good night, Captain."

"Good night, Doctor."

The fire was sputtering slowly down to embers and giving off just a little heat now and less in the way of light. Belly full with a good meal and a decent coffee brewed on the fire, Avci would soon extinguish it altogether and turn in. She had found a tiny cave that was perfect for her purposes. She was fully back in control, a picture of satisfied self-discipline....the boss of every fear and emotion within herself...something her job demanded...and it felt good. She indulged herself in a moment's laughter, then washed, undressed and settled down in her blankets.

The next morning the small force was back on the move. Trys was on horseback but intended to stay visible to his men, his own resilience and determination there to be seen and there to motivate them. He had been pragmatic enough to turn day to day command over to Arden until his recovery was complete, however. Arden was managing admirably, telling his trademark anecdote, this time in his native Spanish, to a Mexican in the company.

"...because I can still play a guitar ,"he finished.

The Mexican broke into a dirty laugh, almost a cackle ,and –forgetting himself-hugged the captain round the shoulder. Arden chuckled and shared a few more words there before he excused himself and went back to directing their journey, all the time offering a word here

,or noticing how things were there ,within the small
private army -and taking action where needed.

o0o

"THAT was amazing…..!"

I blew a long stream of smoke out and felt the
perspiration cooling on me as I sat in the fire exit doorway
of the careworn little backstage area of the college hall.
I was no singer ,I could stay in tune and fake bits of the
vocal styles of my heroes but nothing more. However ,I
had just been inveigled into singing for an impromptu
band as no-one else was feeling sufficiently socially
suicidal, or brave at any rate. I was now on a high and not
regretting doing so one bit!

It had been a buzz too, having to sing and be heard with
two guitarists ,a keyboard and a drumkit, well, be heard
over them in fact! We had cheerfully butchered the single
raising money for the in whose honour the whole
shebang was being held ,as well as a Billy Idol and a
Primitives song. A few compliments had even come my
way afterwards.

There had even been a conversation about being a band.
In that moment the rock and roll dream was hovering
around my consciousness like an alluring phantasmal

53

goddess...by the same time tomorrow reality would probably have hit again! For now, it was nice, however.

I gazed up at the stars and watched them sparkling ,even through the clouds of my cigarette smoke, and wondered briefly if I should be more open to dreams, rather than sometimes simply dismissing them.

I snatched a few hours' sleep at a friend's house before heading home. Over the next week,I slept less and less well at home. Then the local constabulary found me asleep on a bench on the town quay!

I came from being nowhere, unaware, slowly being conscious of hearing voices and feeling cold. My eyes flickered open and I caught sight of wisps of mist swirling and dancing on the river in the light of the early sun and heard the music of its water before I saw two black outlines right there in front of me.

"It's alive, Sarge...."

"So I see," came a reply. Must be Sarge ,I thought.

The other one asked me:

"Where do you live, son?"

"Here."

The policemen came into better focus, at exactly the same moment in which their two frowns suggested this was a bad choice of reply.

"I mean here, as in, this town…"

"Ok. You can have 5 minutes to wake up…then bugger off home, all right?"

I wasn't about to try arguing. The real row was 15 minutes away when I got in, anway!

When I arrived home ,I expected to find myself in trouble. What came unexpected later on that day was a visit from an unknown doctor. I shall be a little more specific: a psychiatrist. I knew I had been difficult, hadn't been sleeping, had been drinking alone at home sometimes and had been reading my usual esoteric and alternative things and writing a few others of my own….but….this?

The Indian doctor was sat right on my parents' sofa, exactly where one of them might sit.The seat of authority, as it were. An expensive suit and shirt were putting up a half decent fight against the physical manifestation of an enjoyment of fine dining, as far as I could see. He glanced up and asked me to sit down ,politely enough but without ceremony. I had deliberately brought a lager in with me.

At some point, after a whole slew of strange questions, he said to me:

"Your parents are concerned because they feel you are interested in some very sinister books and beliefs, almost obsessed, are drinking, possibly using drugs, and that you seem to be heading towards a very self-destructive way of life...."

"Oh right...okay. Well, if I choose to bring about my own destruction ,of any kind, whose business is it as long as I don't harm anyone else?" I asked.

The old guy threw me a look. There was almost a smile in it. Almost. To my pleasant and complete surprise, my reply worked. He was gone five minutes later. Forty minutes later I was back in my room. The visit from the shrink had given me a jolt, though-perhaps not in the way that had been hoped but a jolt nevertheless. That evening I made sure all my coursework was done to date and dragged myself to bed shortly after midnight.

The train journey to college the next day was both subdued and solitary for me. I closed my eyes, and turned one of the silver rings on my fingers whilst I listened to the sounds around me and tried to settle and clear my mind. Arriving there brought further surprises.

"Go on then, we'll record something. What the hell, we'll do it....maybe send it to Peely or someone."

The guitarist from the charity event was stood in front of me, actually saying these words. I surreptitiously pinched myself. Nope, not dreaming according to that, I thought .That evening in a small village hall lit by ageing bulbs that threw a yellowish hue over everything ,we recorded five songs -and probably startled the cattle and ponies in the neighbouring fields and forest respectively.

We'd stolen a drummer from someone(again) and they were pretty good .We still lacked a bass player but that could be done in a crude fashion by programming the keyboard with the bassline. The following morning five copies had been stuffed into Jiffy bags and sent on their way through the postal system to unsuspecting recipients.

The morning air still had a certain crispness to it and it felt quite good to be alive as I walked down the single strip of concrete that made a path through the smoking area from the car park. The students there ,smoking, were the dark or bright patches of their clothes and their animated or neutral faces topped off by plumes of smoke now and then, all painted against the background of the nondescript dirt patch as their bland canvas. Here and there the sun caught the silver of a ring ,earring or bangle amongst the gothics or fell upon some dayglo sock or clothe elsewhere. Every crowd was represented within the little rectangle of dirt where student-kind smoked ,it seemed.

I walked on ,around the sports block, to the prefab that passed for enough of a classroom to hold morning registration and midweek tutor group .I decided that today I was going to do my work and keep quiet-mostly. For no other reason than that is was going to help get me where I felt I belonged ,I was going to work and, in the main ,at least, behave. I drew a breath and pushed the door open.

That evening I took another train home. As I stepped off the train at home and saw the little station lit by its familiar lights, I had not one idea that I was about to oblivious to of the world around me for almost two weeks.

oOo

Trys made his way, aided by crutches, towards the tent where Arden was quartered. As he approached the tent ,he noticed movement further away to the right and saw the captain walk up to the camp perimeter with a local woman, before embracing her and kissing her goodbye. He couldn't see the poor girl in the half-light well but he suspected she was equally as taken with his friend as any of her predecessors. Trys half-smiled to himself. Such things belonged to the past for him. If they made his friend happy and helped him feel more human ,he wasn't about to deny them to him any more. Fair play to him, in short. Arden did need to learn to let them down a bit more gently, perhaps but...that was matter for him.

As Arden neared the tent itself, Trys called out softly.

"Your charm has not deserted you, I see, Raul."

"She was being most insistent, Trys .It would have been unkind to refuse."

"Oh,of course .I suppose at first you had to fend her off and protest all the way too...."

A stunned look took hold of Arden's features.

"What? Make the poor woman think she is not pretty? That would have been TOO unkind!"

Trys sighed loudly. With a resigned shake of his head, he said:

"At least she didn't try to stick you one. We'll call that progress ,shall we ,Captain?"

Avci watched the serving girl walking away as she listened to the exchange with cynical amusement. A sentry lay unconscious at her feet .She had donned his cap, jacket and rifle to disguise herself. A thought crossed her mind again, that same thing noticed once before, before she steered it firmly back to its compartment in her disciplined mind.

Having heard enough for now, she walked calmly away. Once out of sight, she lost the cap and jacket but retained the rifle. A conversation with the girl might be useful, she decided. She hit an easy run, one she could have kept up for miles, and went after her.

The sentry was fortunate enough to wake up without being discovered first but a war at home had taught him the idea of survival first-and he was conspicuously without his weapon and his jacket. When his vision cleared, he quietly stole away into the night himself

....

The child watched her sister clumsily climb the wall round the family farm and drop with equal inelegance , albeit quietly enough, to the ground. Why could she go and see her friends any time? It didn't seem fair.

"Us women, well....we're not really as needy as she makes us look, little one. You might hate me in a moment but just trust me on that much. It will help you in the world."

The words were Farsi and familiar but the accent was strange. A hand went ,firmly but gently, over her mouth and then arms, firm but- once again- kind, plucked her up, pressing her against their owner's chest. A woman! Oh well, thought the child, tonight just got interesting ,at least. Farm life tended to raise pragmatic children with at least one toe in the cold, clear waters of reality.

Meanwhile, the wayward older sister was fast approaching the ground floor window. She knocked softly on the glass, not much noticing the room within but instead glancing nervously behind her. Avci slid the sash window gently upwards and stepped back. She took a second, no more ,to consider her next step. The girl was a bundle of nerves now, all the post amorous glow and

60

outward confidence gone. One word right now and she would be likely to scream.

Sighing in an odd mixture of sympathy and exasperation, Avci tripped her up smartly.As she entered the bedroom. She dropped onto her torso. With her free hand she covered her mouth. Now she could talk herself.

"I have a very reliable, well-maintained British Service Revolver about my person. It would be a shame to need to use it, dear. I doubt you would consider it worth my effort. Is that right?"

The girl nodded frantically. Avci could feel her fear in her tenseness. Catch it in her eyes. Time for a small, calculated risk.

"Good, good all I needed to know. Now, take your baby sister here and sit up on the bed....better. Much better. Now, sparing no detail, tell me alllll about your evening with that bastard and what else you saw there."

The girl glanced nervously at the child, who was watching Avci with growing fascination. The three were pale impressions of their daylight selves in the half moonlight, in a room full of long shadows. Avci laughed softly and knowingly.

"Oh *come onnn*...how many times has she seen the animals out there at it? And anyway, it's a little late for modesty now ,eh? Besides, we won't tell ,will we, little one?"

Later, once she had left the farm way behind her, Avci stopped and then broke into peals of laughter. She was probably that poor farm girl's worst nightmare....tell me allll about it....no, it was no good, she was off laughing again! Managing to contain herself for a moment ,she recalled some more things, this time from the girl's account. Oh no, no, no, no girl, you simply did NOT do things that way! Once again she was laughing. Eventually her laughter subsided. Then her face set hard and expressionless. A dose of reality now would help both those girls later in life ,she said to herself. She had done them a favour ,in actual fact ,and hadn't killed them either. There were things to do-and people to harry, maybe even kill. She set out to find her contact.

....

Elsewhere, Trys was sat at a folding map table. The maps were long since put away, however, and the next strategic step planned. He was now poring over books that pertained to what Arden called his little hobby. Arden shared a mother tongue with some of the men and had gone to spend some time with them before turning in. A raucous laugh minutes later suggested that The Captain had mopped up one of the last few people already met that hadn't heard his jokes.

Now, Trys was sat, apparently staring into space. His eyes were totally vacant now, however. His breathing was slow, measured and regular. Wherever his essence was right that moment, it was unaware of the immediate surroundings in the tent. It was some time before he returned to such an awareness, ate a little and made some tea, before turning in.

....

Lieutenant Kitchener-Crane really didn't need this taking place on his tour of duty. Whoever these men were ,they had all the manners of bandits in their style of combat. His CO was already dead a few feet away, felled by a single bullet shot from some way off. That simply was not something a gentleman did. Damn it, he would too say it to himself, it was NOT cricket!

Worse still, that left him in charge. Sadly for his opponents, however, Kitch , as his friends called him, had grown up an army brat of the British Empire and had already seen fighting styles the world over. Yes, he might have been a little spoilt by Nanny and Mama but he was otherwise very much a realist and a bright young man with it. He had clocked the American Civil War sniper's tactic from his own reading. He took a breath and turned to the other survivors. HIS men now. He looked around the little mud fort that guarded the godforsaken highway and saw the expectation and trust in their expressions. He could do this. He must. He owed them nothing less. His King and his country expected nothing less.

"Right! These bastards are fighting like tribal savages or bandits, not soldiers as you understand them. Those who do know how, respond accordingly. The rest of you, watch them and learn. Be wary of making yourself a target for their snipers. They lack manners. On my signal, fire at will! Good luck men- and GOD SAVE THE KING!!"

Away from the fort, things almost immediately began to take a decided turn for the worse for Trys and Arden. Some dandy with a revolver had just appeared out of nowhere at the top of the buliding, picked two of the men off as they tried their luck on the wall, then disappeared fast. Most people couldn't make those kinds of shots with a pistol for toffee. That was concerning enough. Worse still, however, others amongst the British were now conserving ammunition , saving more rounds for taking careful shots rather than firing wildly. The machine gunner ,too, had gone from sweeping his fire across the whole field to firing bursts.

Seen in outline, against the strong sun, one mercenary went spinning, just like a marionette. His rifle flew far from him, from his silhouette, even as they watched. He was done for, even before he hit the ground. Somewhere within the tiny mud fort a voice was audible giving orders now and then, in calm, clear, received pronunciation and without wavering or faltering. Oh how very British, thought Trys, with a slight sneer. As a former British officer himself, however, he knew all too well that that same unflabbable calm would ,in itself ,be helping the men's morale. And well, come to think of it, hadn't some

Puritan thinker said something about a nation fonder of servitude than of freedom right after the English Civil War too?

Well, there would be time for philosophising later ,if they all survived. Trys made a fast assessment. They were losing men too quickly. It was that simple. He turned to Arden.

"Whoever is in charge now knows what he's about. We're here for Señor Dinero ,my friend, the money, not King and Country. Remind the men of that and then call the retreat, please, Captain."

Throwing a few grenades and a little fire to cover themselves, as well as the odd curse or insult in a mixture of mother tongues, the mercenary band withdrew. A ragged cheer went up from the fort as the realisation that they had won the day hit them. Enjoy it, gentlemen, thought Trys. It might not last.

Trys need not have expended too much thought on the matter, after all, as it turned out. A dispatch received later that evening recalled Kitch and his men to England. The fort was to be abandoned back to the whims of local chieftains . There was fighting to be done in France and in Flanders.....

....

Avci had watched the whole thing with a fair amount of interest, some amusement and not a little grudging admiration for the British officer. He should be thankful that circumstances put them on the same side. Otherwise, well....he would have had to go.

Her contact had left her fairly well updated, as well as slightly irritated. The hood and the hushed voice were the sort of theatrics that ,frankly, annoyed her intensely in business meetings of any kind. Show your face,at least, or else send someone who does. Still, no matter. Her own apparent composure and failure to be spooked by said theatrics seemed to have unsettled him. Good. He had also brought her an absolutely beautiful Mauser rifle. Very good. A slight shiver of anticipation went through her. She was looking forward to using it properly. Doing so now fit her further instructions from her employer too.

She dropped into a firing posture and sighted on one of the stragglers of the band. Regulated her breathing correctly. Squeezing the trigger gently, incrementally ,she waited for the pressure to become just enough to trip the firing mechanism. A hundred metres away, the straggler fell.

Now she must move-and fast. Rolling away from the lip of the ledge, she swung over its edge. Letting both hands go she fell into a crouch at the head of a small gulley and ran. After a short while, she fell back into her easy jog and kept going until she was well and truly out of the way.

....

The men had been mollified , eventually, with a promise to deal with their unwelcome shadow (permanently) and the offer of a reward for anyone who brought them into camp with evidence-and alive, if possible. The fact that their skins had already been saved by the retreat hadn't hurt either. Seeing their comrade paid for taking out Kitch's CO sealed the matter. This man Trys kept to his end of a bargain ,clearly.

Avci was sat barely a mile away, now dressed as an eccentric European aristocrat. The hired muscle glaring at passersby for sheer enjoyment kept unwanted attention away, for the most part. They had two things in common. They were Turks. They were killers for hire. That was enough to forge an understanding. In a few minutes, Avci would also earn her countryman's respect, although for now he was happy enough to simply take her money. A shadow fell across her table at the little inn, or little whatever-this-place-actually-was.

"Excuse me, do we know you? You look as though you hail from more civilised parts and Jonno and I thought we knew already everyone in this godforsaken hole."

An immaculately turned out and rather pretty young Englishwoman was looking down at her, a similarly well-presented man at her side. Ah, these would do.

"I am called the Countess Maria Fernanda de Alcanzar," said Avci with a nod and a charming smile.

"I confess to a love of adventure, which is something I hope to find out here, away from the fighting," she continued.

"Well, I'm Kitty Stubbington and this, er, this is Jonno of course...we're out here with my father. He's the military governor," offered the young woman.

Avci gave Kitty a very direct look and said:

"Oh now, that DOES sound very exciting. I like excitement, don't you? Would you like to join me, Kitty? I do enjoy some intelligent conversation. Imir here is a good retainer but he speaks little."

Kitty glanced at her brother who offered only a slight shrug in response. As his sister sat down with the other girl, he decided to chance his luck.

" I shall be at your service later ,Countess ,if you need anything," he ventured.

"That is so very kind of you but I couldn't *possibly* and besides ,I have a feeling that Kitty and I will have so very much to keep us....occupied. With Imir around, we are perfectly safe, sir. I shall see to it that your sister is escorted home safely. My word on it."

Jonno Stubbington gave a curt nod. He could have insisted-but he had a feeling that would end badly, awkwardly. His sister could be so very headstrong at times herself. If the Spaniard was indeed an aristo that would add potential diplomatic complications to matters, what was more. His imagination failed to help him further, however, either in his own true intentions or realising what Avci's actually were.

"Ladies," he murmured, with a practised smile ,as a way of excusing himself.

Avci was feeling good and already had some personal entertainment in mind. Entertainment of a very different kind to that of the other night . What was more ,it would probably aid her in achieving her objectives more quickly . She could easily have targeted the brother and enjoyed her entertainment just as much but hey, a little variety never hurt.

....

Sometime before dawn two mornings later, a figure stood before the fort, now a home to tribal fighters put there by the local warlord. drawing in deep breaths and taking in the deep darkness of the pre-dawn scene ,it closed its eyes and began to whisper softly. The whisper grew in volume but never broke into anything that could be heard at a distance.

Tongues of flame, half seen, began to appear, will o' the wisp-like just above the surface of the ground close to the fort. They began to dance, almost, coalescing into an ever-intensifying, ever growing circle of fire. the heat began to be a real thing, warming the cool night air. Shadows danced too in the firelight ,round and about the shape of the fort. The heat intensified, the circle exploded to a sphere, engulfing the fort.

A few screams, some exploding munitions that added to the terrible display were the only sounds and then the fireball imploded with a pop, almost comically, leaving glowing rubble, mere bricks and embers, and the dead.

The figure slumped, half-exhausted. Righting itself a few moments later, it offered a small bow of respect- surprisingly-in the direction of the destroyed building before turning and walking away at a measured pace.

A few hours later, a caravan of pack animals and their owners passed down the highway and past the scene. A caravan belonging to friends of a certain Osman.

....

"Barely a trickle got through, sir. Certainly not enough to make a significant difference."

"Trickle, you say? What got through before was a trickle....this was a blasted river....that new Ministry will have my commission and my post for this!"

Stubbington senior saw the look of dejection on the young adjutant's face after his outburst and sighed inwardly.

"Never mind, man. Never mind. Let's look at what CAN be done, shall we? Find my son and the others and let's get to work!"

"Yes, sir!" the adjutant replied, saluting smartly.

Stubbington smiled wearily and returned the salute . His daughter was having afternoon tea with that Countess again. The Lord could indeed show mercy at times. She was a super girl, top but he felt certain her dear mother had trained her up on how to nag him and boss him about. Perhaps he could have fifteen minutes peace now ,if only to work out what the hell he was going to do here.

o0o

"This is like being in hell," I told them.

The place was all battleship greys, hospital greens and sturdy hardwood doors with meaningfully stout locks and fire exit circles in bureaucratic blue. A sickly yellow light cast its pall over all of these other things from the fluorescent lights, which were themselves trapped behind white wire-mesh covers.

Apparently, I had been brought here after freaking out at home for three days solid. I remembered little, something hazy ,perhaps, but no more than that. Worse still, my parents had signed off on this! I was stuck here.

I passed the tray back to the girl in the nursing uniform and invited them to screw themselves every one. I retreated to the bed I had emerged from minutes before. It was my only home and a makeshift escape for a few days more. I let sleep claim me anew.

oOo

The Ottoman captain lay face down in the dirt and hoped to be taken for dead. He kept his ears open and shuddered as he recalled the last hour or so. A couple of trucks, those confounded things with the new internal combustion engines, had rumbled down the road, toward them, spooking both men and horses-then opened fire! The vehicles had ploughed on, shooting. They had rained bullets and grenades. Screaming men, panicked horses....then snipers began taking out individual men.

Next, mounted men had ridden up and done their worst, hacking and shooting. Then, mercenaries on foot had either stabbed or shot the rest of his men to death. He had never known the like. He hoped he lived to never have to repeat the experience. He swore to the Almighty that if he did so, if he survived, he would become a simple shopkeeper or bar owner back in Istanbul.

A shadow fell over him. Avci looked down at his sprawled figure, once again in her black killer's clothing, her rifle over one shoulder and the stolen service revolver in one hand. She smiled slightly to herself before she spoke.

"Get up, man! We're countrymen, so I think I shall let you live. Don't mess me about though. I have work to do."

The captain opened an eye warily and ,finding himself still alive having done so, got carefully to his feet. The Almighty had sent help very quickly, he thought. Bar or shop it was. Whoever this was, however, she didn't fit his idea of a saving angel very well.

"What do you want with me?" he croaked ,his mouth and throat quite dry.

"Who did this?"

"Mercenaries...they came at us like demons....trucks ,then cavalry, then....it was terrible! Terrible!"

"All right, sweetie , all right. Thanks! You can go now. Don't dawdle! I get bored soooo quickly."

He needed no further prompting. Ten paces on there was a horse that had returned. He took the reins, uttered soothing sounds, making sure the beast looked calm enough now as he did so ,pulled thirstily on a water bottle in the saddlebag and then was off in a trail of hoofbeats and dust.

Five hours later a large but otherwise unremarkable-looking caravan, made up of camels and the odd donkey, ambled past the sorry scene and on down the highway. The pack animals were heavily-laden yet well-fed and cared for. Their cargo of contraband was on its way through the obstacles that had so irked Osman's cartel.

....

"Have you seen him like this before, Captain?"

"Oh yes, it happens to him now and then when he has been at his little hobby."

"Little hobby....?"

"Doctor, it would put you in a happier place to remain ignorant."

"Very well," said the Russian doctor, "in which case I recommend a little of this and lot more rest. He recovers extremely well from the leg wound. This may set him back though, whatever it is."

They roused Trys enough to take the doctor's draught , then let him fall back into the folds of his blankets. After the Doctor left, Raul Arden glanced nervously, almost warily, around before calling out.

"You can come out of hiding, whoever you are. One bad move and I am going to kill you, ok?"

Avci froze in the back of the tent. This one was still good, she thought with grudging admiration.

"Hello Raul....it's been a very, very long time."

Avci moved the material covering her face aside. At the sight of her face the captain broke into a laugh.

"Ohhh , it's you, is it, my sister?"

"HALF sister, Raul dearest, let's not muddy the waters right out. Well, I can't kill you. Much though it might please me to. I promised our mother. I guess we shall just have to talk instead," Avci told him.

She looked down at Trys' sleeping form with cold, professional interest. Asked what had happened. Ah, yes, he would live, she could already see that: the colour was already seeping back into his features. So be it. To her, like them, this was work, nothing personal .

Arden switched to Spanish. Asked her what she wanted. A deal, she replied and she indicated that she would feel awkward killing his friend so a deal was better for all three of them. If you managed it was the gist of his reply. He asked her what did she have in mind. She told him. He shook his head, laughing softly . He said that she had learned, had she not. She conceded that she had had a good teacher.

After Avci left, her brother looked down at his friend with a look of concern and affection. First checking the tent, he drew out an old rosary and began to pray it more fervently than he ever had in his life.

oOo

I had eventually emerged from the bed where I hid. I was now looking out over lawn whose landscaped slope looked out over the sea. Behind the silhouettes of redwood branches I could make out waves sent sparkling by the afternoon sun and hear the occasional sound from the beach some way beneath ,the call of one person to another or the shriek of a child….excited sounds from the everyday world that seemed so very out of place in this strange, enforced tranquillity in which I found myself prisoner.

The shape of a head blotted out the sight of the sea. A face grinned into mine.

"Got a spare fag, please ,mush?"

This again. I sighed and passed them a cigarette. I was running out fast but had more on the way, thankfully.

"Thanks! Owe you one."

"Yeah ,cool, yeah…"

Trys was now looking at the Chinese merchant with increasing impatience. He had not asked why the fellow was out here trading and he did not really care, for that matter. Then again, they had been trying to strike a deal for the last two hours. It was said that you could get anything here ,if you were willing to pay. Trys began to doubt it. This might be the very latest thing but he had limits and it was not an absolute essential .He finally opted for one of the oldest tricks known to a frustrated potential buyer ,that is, he spun on his heel and made to walk off.

"All right ,all right, pay Sterling, pay dollar ,pay gold, aircraft is yours."

"Captain….this man of ours…he really can fly one of these things, I hope? This contraption isn´t exactly going for a song."

"Oh yes, sir ! He learnt it last year helping some… friends….in the Somme .I had that checked before we left. His story appears true. He himself says it's incredible being in the sky! There is nothing like it."

"Wonderful…..well, he now has a Spad Seven biplane to make friends with. Next attack, he's first in ,before the lorries. Let's find him somewhere flat for an airfield first, though."

The biplane, still in its original French racing green and red , a model already famous for being simple yet effective and deadly was being now moved by harassed staff and a small team of oxen. The sight of such a jarring clash of the very old and very new made Trys smile briefly to himself.

………….

The Mexican cackled. The Spad flew in fast, nose tilting down. Its Vickers gun opened up. Men and horses scattered under its flight path, fleeing the gunfire, or trying to. The shadow fell across them ,passed, was gone, then came back for another pass. The pilot kept this up until his ammunition was spent.

The company tried to pull itself together. As it did so, a distant sound of other engines grew nearer, grew stronger. Two trucks came round a corner of the terrain and down the dusty highway. Shots burst from them. Then grenades rained from them. Horses threw their riders, panicked anew. Some men simply fled now. The air smelled of cordite and fear. It was full of sounds too.

Shouts . Shots ringing out. Shrieks from horses .
Explosions.

The trucks ploughed through the ravaged company,
stopping for nothing, and carried on down the highway.
The scene was beginning to calm a little once again. A
shot rang out. The company commander fell down , dead.

By the time the horses and the first foot soldiers came
into sight the trickle of fleeing men was gaining strength,
becoming a rout. Still more were killed as they fled. This
was war waged without mercy. Another window of
opportunity now lay open for Osman's friends.

…………..

"Well, my guess would be that news of us had spread.
This isn't the kind of company we were looking for
,though. When it gets to close quarters, we'll have our
work cut out. Get the Spad armed and up there…now
,please, Captain .That will give him time for a second run.
Stress the gravity of the situation to him too."

"Sir!"

The telescope was showing Trys an image he had not
wanted to see. A well-turned out but very-businesslike -
looking couple of companies of the British Indian Army
with Gurkha mercenaries in their ranks were moving
steadily in their direction. He did not want to use his
other talents right here and now either. That would have
to wait. Swearing violently to himself ,he went to fetch

one of the sniper Lee Enfields . As he did so, the Spad went overhead ,its engine audible ,its shadow falling across him like the silhouette of some avenging demoness off to join a celestial fray. The Mexican would probably be in full song right now, he knew. As long as he hit home with the Vickers gun he could deliver a dozen music hall numbers ,for all Trys cared.

Trys settled into his firing position. This fellow was a major, from the looks of his sleeve insignia. Perhaps Trys should feel honoured. His mind took a detour at that point. As he thought of one detail from his own time as an officer, memories, images, and other things from his posting to Dublin crept in. Angrily,he clawed his thoughts back to the present .

Aim for his middle first. Biggest target area. Focus….concentrate….breathe in….half out…squeeze ,don't pull…..he could hear his old instructor´s words as though he was still in Great Marlow. The Lee Enfield kicked his shoulder, hard. The sound was loud, raw. The major jerked like a startled puppet, then fell half-forwards, across his horse. To the beast's credit, it didn't startle or bolt.

At that moment the biplane swooped in and began to rain bullets on the soldiers below. The timing, though not planned, was almost perfect. Trys watched with some admiration. The man could indeed fly that thing. He was now performing a perfect manoeuvre now and heading back for a second pass. They might just get away with this. Just…. He went now to resume full command.

A crack, a bullet, whipped past him. He threw himself flat. Strained to hear anything different above the sounds of the Spad finshing its first run. He would wait a moment and keep his senses alert for anything closer at hand. Having done that, he headed off at a crouched run, the Enfield loaded but across his back.

A figure appeared on the path, swathed in black and with its face covered, veiled, a Mauser rifle held lightly, almost casually, yet very much ready, at its hip. Trys noted a revolver stuck in a belt and several knives too. He didn´t exactly have time for this. Still, nor did he have much choice. He was watching the figure carefully and weighing his options when it spoke.

"Don´t worry ,dear," said a woman´s voice " I just wanted to see you closer for myself. It amuses me for His Majesty´s British Indian Army to fail this once, so I intend to help you see to it. After today…..hmm, well! Have a wonderful afternoon, Colonel!"

She bowed half-mockingly and was gone.

As the Spad quit the field of battle, a growing sound of hoofbeats could be heard. From the edges of the valley, from both sides of it, the sound grew stronger. Shortly afterwards, the silhouettes of horsemen broke the skyline on both sides and stayed there a brief moment ,both to menace with their presence and to survey the scene. One local tribal chieftain truly despised the British and their influence-or as he saw it, their unwelcome meddling- in his corner of the world. To the abyss with treaties! After a tip off, he had chosen today to act. His whole band of fighters were here. He had also found others who were prepared to come along to the fight. Today he would send their King and their Prime Minister a message.

The riders plunged over the sides of the valley , two thundering waves of warriors about to crash mercilessly into each flank of the two companies. Steel blades flashed here and there in the sun as they came on and the first few gunshots broke out from both sides. The sound of the aircraft could be heard again too, the ominous sound of its engine drawing near. Its machine gun opened up, the aircraft´s dipped nose raining rounds on the soldiers below .Its pilot had enough initiative to target the infantry and not the incoming riders.

The tribesmen and many of the British troops fell into bloody hand-to hand fighting as horses startled and close quarters left no time to reload. Trys was now applying his own shock tactics too. Trucks and carriages had made their initial sorties and now his men were harrying the British before retreating ,then harrying once again and withdrawing once more.

When ,eventually, the British called a retreat, many of their Gurkhas only complied rather than disobey orders. The tribesmen troubled them for a few minutes more before themselves leaving the field of battle and disappearing into the surrounding hills. Trys´men were already well out of it. Avci watched from her foxhole and considered her next move. Her half brother had better keep his bloody mouth shut, if only to avoid making her more work. He needed to remember their arrangement too. After a moment´s consideration, she felt more confident that he would keep his word . They both had guts and self-discipline aplenty. He had, unfortunately, also been struck down with having principles at any early age.

o0o

They had given up trying to get me to do jolly group activities and let me write in the end. I had also taken to exploring the gardens. I had even found an old brass plaque in a flowerbed that commemorated the place being a wartime hospital for American airmen and stuck it on show on a window sill so all could see.

I still felt trapped, imprisoned but it had become hell with nice grounds now. There were still traces of a landscaped mansion garden and the odd hint of perfume in the sea air here and there from a surviving rose or fragrant shrub. Somewhere beyond the wall of redwood and pine trees the sea could be heard and- if you walked right to the edge of the garden -even seen in glimpses of sparkling blue waves.

o0o

"We'll march by night, move quietly. There should be enough of a breech in things here to let trade through with only the enforcers in the caravans themselves to do any fighting, as long as they're careful . This time tomorrow we'll be well into Afghanistan. Find me here at 1930 hours. Let's catch what sleep we may first. Oh and sir?"

The Russian doctor ministering to Trys gave a slight start. The Colonel had just called Arden sir. Arden merely turned round to and look expectantly at his friend.

"That blasted assassin came to find me. To see me for herself ,she said. We need to do something about her."

"You may consider it in hand ,colonel."

Arden threw a perfect salute, turned on his heel and left.

"You didn't hear anything out of the ordinary there, did you, Dr Poborsky?"

The other man first answered with a faint smile, then said:

"I am a doctor. Since Hypocrates' time we have guarded our patient's secrets jealously ,sir."

"Good. Good man. What will you do when this is over?"

"I will go to America and practice medicine. If I never see any more war ,it will be too soon ,frankly ,sir. And you?"

"I shall carry on as I have begun. There will always be work for my kind. Always. The Captain was an officer in the Spanish navy, incidentally, before he became my second in command. I left the Army as a lieutenant colonel, before they could send me to France to be hated , like I´m told any other staff officer is, by those poor bastards in the trenches. Captain Arden ,for his part, preferred to to die on terra firma. He was born on it, he would die on it, he told me. I value his experience and his knowledge. He values mine. He once outranked me ,technically. Hence he gets sir now and again, in private."

There was a rare compassion in Trys´voice, seldom heard, that touched the doctor. He finished his work, cleaned up and made ready to leave. He paused at the exit.

"Good night, sir. The Army lost an asset when they lost you, if forgive me saying it."

…………

"Boss, boss, soldiers!! We will be rich again…and maybe I will get a new sister!"

The little rascal ran straight in, like always , and then stood gawping -and slightly breathless -at the sight of Imir´s boot on the head of the chief´s guard. Then he took in the woman herself –she was beautiful, so pretty - and found himself captivated like some mesmerised rodent. The chief, Anushiravan ,glared at the lad and - despite the scene-began to bellow.

"Stop staring , you son of a-"

And there he stopped himself. The common insult , son of a whore ,was perhaps too close to the bone for this particular boy. His face didn´t change a bit but the longstanding affection in his heart flickered to life ,momentarily. He lowered his voice and tempered its tone.

"Relax, Amardad . Business. This lady is our guest. If she wanted me dead, well, one of us already would be. Her man is just having a difference of opinion with Isfandier. You know how men of their profession are, boy! Thank you for the news. Now get lost, you little scoundrel!"

Amardad was startled at this unaccustomed display of manners towards him from the boss . The man was a daily surprise. Still, maybe that´s how he stayed boss….. He muttered a cheeky comment under his breath and left.

"What a little sweetie. Says it how he sees it. I find real honesty in men in such a rare thing, don´t you , Chief?"

The Countess was back in play. Avçi smiled up from her seat. HIS seat , dammit! A sensible long skirt, boots and jacket had replaced the outfits from her previous appearances elsewhere. The voice was delivered to sound carefully cultured .The smile suggested warmth. There was something in her eyes and that same voice, though, that told Anushiravan to leave this one alone, to give her whatever it was actually she wanted and then get her the hell out of his village. He still wouldn´t miss an opportunity to make her pay for crossing him ,however, should one be granted him, of course....at the exact moment he thought this, the smile vanished from the woman´s face.

"Business ,yes, back to that," she was saying .She continued:

" A man will come this way with his mismatched private army. There are fewer of them now than there were. His deputy will pay you a visit for supplies. You are to detain him, his deputy. I will see to the rest myself. This is all I need from you. Is it a deal?"

"If it gets you gone, woman, it is," he growled.

Avçi laughed delightedly. He really didn´t like her, did he? Well, tough, he´d have to get used to her being around for a day or two.

"Oh, come now , don´t be so sullen, Chief. I will also pay you well for it."

After the Countess had left, taking her tame lion bodyguard with her, he turned to his own man .

"Don´t feel any shame, brother, we live. We´re both realists. You did your duty in my book. I have plans for that smug bitch though. Now,this is how we are going to do it.....”

....

“I´m a little uncertain as to how I can help you, Admiral....?”

“Guiterrez , your Excellency, Admiral Guiterrez.”

“Right. Would you care to elaborate?”

“You were having a killer operating in your jurisdiction. We trained....them...well , mostly it was His Majesty´s Armada,the one that trained them, at any rate. Where they are, in our experience, their brother is never far away. Their brother *was* one of our finest officers... that´s another matter, flour from another sack, so to speak. We want his sibling . They have questions to answer for us. “

The change in the man´s tone and the light behind his eyes as he spoke the last two sentences told Stubbington that ´they´ would not enjoy the quiz much. The men of His Majesty´s Armada were hard men in his experience. They might be famous back in England for the wrong reasons, for a fleet that got shipwrecked off Ireland but in person they were usually quite formidable. They came from a tradition much more used to hand to hand fighting than that of his own colleagues in His Majesty´s Navy. The British approach was a more tactical one, which relied far more on its commanders and technological clout. The Spanish one was from a history of sailors more wont to board, have at you and be done with it. A bit too piratical for his own liking but undeniably effective , given the right circumstances.

"Okay, Admiral. Pull up a chair, sir. I´m listening."

....

....

Sergeant Abstinence Thorpe sat sullenly cleaning his scavenged rifle and mourning his lot. Since stealing away from disgracing himself as a sentry, he had fallen back on every trick he had learned on the streets of Leeds and on the fields of France and Flanders. Luckily, that same box of tricks had gifted him more than a weighted deck or a white rabbit. He was clothed, fed and armed now. The Colonel or that….woman….was going to pay for his shame. He needed only to decide which one.

The thought had him start to smile. A little whistle took life upon his lips. He worked the now expertly oiled bolt on the weapon. She was only a Russian infantry weapon but that made her sturdy. Practical and useful. Just like Abs Thorpe. Yes indeed. Well, without his brilliant humour but you could not have everything, could you?

He shouldered her and took aim at a row of stolen beer bottles. He´d drunk their contents first. Those of a few more as well. Insult to the brewer not to, he felt. No fool, he had deliberately messed up the sniper trial as he had wanted to lead a few of the men himself.

Bang...bottle one blew....bang....then two...bang ,oh, look....three....bang....four....bang....five ...

Hee hee hee....time to reload? Maybe. Maybe not.

"Halt....Who goes there?" said Thorpe with a chuckle.

"Friend or foe?"

"Hey, Colonel, can you tell yer 792 from yer 303....tee hee hee..."

By now he was indeed cackling gleefully. He had taken out all five bottles ,though drunk as a lord. If he got close, Trys or Avçi would need more than prayers and magic. They would need to see him coming .

He heard footsteps. They wanted to be quiet. He was a soldier. He had heard them underneath his own noise. Two robed figures seemed put out that he was watching them expectantly as they broke cover into the clearing. Even so, they wasted no time.

"Good Afternoon, soldier. Would you be available to play someone´s ...er...well, call it...minder and guardian angel, please? From a distance. Our Conclave will pay you verrrry well…"

"Oh, aye? And who might you be, flouncing around in a frock all the way out here? Oberon the bloomin´ fairy king?"

An immaculately shaved face offered a polite but forced smile in response to the reference to his robes, whilst the face of the other was fighting not to show mirth behind its beard.

"Oh we know of lord Oberon, yes, yes…we do so love ancient literature ourselves, friend but we´re not his men. From you, well , we need only an answer, please."

"Then yes. You two give me the heebie-jeebies , mind but you´re paying. Let´s have some of the money now , though and no clever games. Then we have a deal."

After money had changed hands and the two had then left, Thorpe levelled the seemingly empty rifle at a spare water bottle off to his right.

A shot. The bottle was holed and leapt.

"One up the spout for luck, sir!"

More laughter: except that now there was much more of a sense of purpose and much less insanity to it.

……………………………..

Avçi paid the girl and thanked her. Oh dear, such a disappointment , some of these so-called leaders and chiefs of men. Still, betrayal was common enough currency out here, much as it had been in Istanbul. She had planned with contingencies in place for it already .There did, however, appear to be a section of British soldiers and her former commanding officer, as he probably viewed himself ,anyhow, approaching. Now that item of news really *was* inconvenient. Still, this second kind of development actually helped keep a little spice in a girl´s life, she told herself.

Outside in the distance a disgruntled British Corporal was about to be challenged unexpectedly. It would do little for his own mood but it would be hugely entertaining for the other protagonist.

"Halt! Who goes there?"

The figure had put itself with the sun at its back. The accent was British ,broad and northern.

Reigning in his walking horse, the corporal squinted down. Took in the stripes and crown rank insignia. This wasn´t wanted. This was another complication to his already overcomplicated day. Technically, he was looking at a senior NCO.

"Corporal Goldman of His Majesty´s Army. Who am I addressing?"

The figure moved more fully into view. A well-presented staff sergeant, in fact, his colonial uniform beautifully ironed and buffed, his boots shining brightly. He carried an unusual-looking rifle.

" You and His army, eh? His Majesty, our beloved King. Sergeant Abs Thorpe, of the same."

Thorpe glanced at the small squad. Guiterrez and Thorpe´s eyes met in that moment. Thorpe took in the uniform. Both knew trouble when they saw it. Thorpe saw an intelligent but deadly operator beneath the careful shield of cultured Cadiz airs and graces, Guiterrez that Thorpe was far from the clown he made out, a survivor of the worst that life could throw at one.

"Sergeant….a word alone, please. If I may, of course, corporal?"

"Yes sir. My orders are to assist you, and- therefore -of course ,"replied the unhappy corporal.

Guiterrez dismounted, loosening the flap on his holster as he did so. Oh this should be good, thought Thorpe .A minute or two later they were some way out of earshot of the other men.

"I´ll cut to the chase….sergeant….." said the admiral in tones which conveyed the fact that he suspected the other was less than a legitimate operator. "I suspect you are not willing to let us pass. Answer me one thing and I will let that happen for you."

"Oh aye? Anything else in it for me?"

"Only that I don´t deal with you afterwards. Personally."

Thorpe tipped him a nod in consent.

"Your question."

"The person you are guarding is female and calls herself a Spanish Countess. Yes or no?"

"Aye, that she does. Yes."

"Thank you. We will leave now."

To Thorpe´s utter amazement, the admiral saluted sharply. He returned it reflexively in his surprise-and turning on their respective heels, they went their separate ways.

……………………………………………..

By the time Guiterrez had got back to Stubbington´s residence, a messenger had also arrived from the slighted village chieftain to let him know of the plan to detain Arden. At that moment Arden was walking down a dusty track ,surprised to find himself in the middle of fields of growing ,living and very enthusiastically thriving poppies .

Their purple flowers brought a splash of colour to the scenery as they danced in the breeze blowing down from the surrounding hills. Clouds punctuated the blue skies but the day was warm, even hot, the sun bursting out through them often. A truck rumbled along behind him before he waved it past. They would wait for him. As the land began to rise ,so he turned into the little road to the village itself and kept walking briskly. He heard hurried steps behind, went to his belt, went to turn...and went out like a light, struck down, unconscious, as he started to turn.

He came to in darkness. Theatrics followed: the flare of a match told him his beloved sister had kept to her end of the deal. The grinning Englishman was an added surprise, however. Where the hell *was* Avçi now?

"Aren´t we the lucky one, Capitán? Her ladyship has a soft spot for you ,it seems."

"Ha! If only you knew.....Story of my blasted life!"

He asked for coffee and it was forthcoming but....a five year old could have brewed better. Still ,the smell of the beans filling the small space of the tent was heartening and welcome. He was beginning to cheer up when the village chieftain walked in and looked him up and down. He met the man´s eyes with a calm like the Mediterranean on a windless morning .A calm that spoke, nonetheless , of the ever-present possibility of a storm.

"It´s all right, your chiefliness ,I ´ve already mentioned what a lucky fella he is," Thorpe put in.

"Gentleman, I´ll cut straight to the chase….any chance we can kill this bitch?" said the chieftain in very passable English.

Despite himself, Arden was quietly laughing. Thorpe, however, now lost his humorous air. He held his counsel however.

"I´m sorry ,I can´t do that, Chief...I have outstanding business with her that needs her alive."

"Me too," added Thorpe.

The atmosphere soured now-and quickly-and was peppered with a very black set of Persian curses from the chief.

Ten minutes later, however, whilst listening to Abs Thorpe´s account of events, Avçi´s delighted laugh split the air like the flying arrows of some mischievous deity.

"You have a way of telling things, Sergeant….that´s for certain," she said when her peals of laughter finally stilled .

She glanced at Arden before continuing.

"Guiterrez is in these parts. Thankfully some unfriends of your Colonel hired me this fellow. Seems he saw the Admiral off," she told him.

"Oh ho, I see…this explains your state of mood….erm, one moment ,Sergeant. Forgive us- but what you don´t know , can´t hurt you."

A hurried conversation in Spanish followed, terminated by her a curse in Turkish from Avçi. There was another bargain struck. Thorpe himself could tell that ,as he watched them like a parody of a spectator at lawn tennis. The curse was more from exasperation.

"Try it. It works. I mean ,don´t shoot yourself….that´s too much of a chance to take …but….it works," added Avçi in English.

Ooh, thought Thorpe to himself, I hope Oberon the Jessie keeps me on the payroll. This gets better by the minute. Then the serious look settled over his features, the one with the lad behind it that had clawed his way up from and out of the streets of Leeds, into the Army and from there to true adventure, as he saw it anyway, that is : into the world of the soldier of fortune.

o0o

I was back with the Indian guy again.

"So are you a real doctor?"

"Well, yes, we have to spend the seven years in medical school first before we train in psychiatry. So, yes. Though I have only practiced as a psychiatrist for some years now,of course."

"How many people do you cure, then...?"

o0o

Trys looked out through a glassless window in the ruins, which had a silhouette pleasingly close to that of an ox carcass. He looked at the approaching men. A small detachment of British . Let them come. The men would follow their instructions ,their orders. Their greed would see to that. For now, at least. He had struck camp once Arden had not returned . After that, he had moved the band here. Finishing a very welcome tea, he closed his eyes and contemplated.

 He was sat there several hours later, just having some biscuits and South American coffee, when the prisioners were brought in. The smell of coffee was there still, hovering, enticing and inviting the senses to wake up to its presence. As was the smell of fear. Three embarrassed looking and bruised British soldiers and a composed Spanish naval officer –composed, maybe but also with an air of fury controlled by strong will to him.

To the Mexican ,who had led them in, he said:

"Lieutenant, thank you. Please give your bird some exercise tomorrow for me. Give this gentleman opportunity to make himself some coffee...he will enjoy this blend, I expect.He and I, we have things to discuss.

"As for you blaggards," he said with a nod to the British "I have a proposition. You can join us, follow orders and fit in, or you can be shot at dawn. Up to you. Let my NCO know at that time. Good day to you."

"Alejandro Magno….Alexander The Great. One of his favourite recruitment tactics, was this, I believe…."

"Indeed. Nothing like a little quiet contemplation time to bring….inspiration"

The others were herded out.

"Haven´t seen you since…Cairo and our meeting with Thomson. How are you, sir?"

"Better, now that I am given to make my own coffee. Your countrymen always ruin good coffee, Trys."

"Just so we´re clear, I never discuss those…Cairo… matters , nor those of the Conclave , in these circles we´re in at this moment."

 "Understood. I walk in my ancestors footsteps Trys…and mine fooled Torquemada himself."

Trys smiled and then laughed softly. Guiterrez continued:

"So,a long time that I have heard nothing of you ,Colonel. How are you…and how do we resolve all this?"

o0o

Outside in the car park the needlessly bright light, at least one needlessly bright to my mind, cast a garish yellow glow over the small huddle of parked cars . The cars themselves seemed like a small herd of beasts keeping close for warmth on a cold night. I smiled briefly at my own imagination-and then, it suddenly struck me....

Pressing my back to the paint, plaster and brick of the old corridor,I felt its cool and ,breathing slow ,let myself drift. Some hours later, I stirred, caught a cup of coffee off the last of the hot drinks trolleys doing the rounds as I headed back to the dorm and went off to record my thoughts.

o0o

"Great hairy pillocks!!" said Stubbington, in shock ,in horror. Throwing himself to the floor, he heard a machine gun, heard glass spray inwards .He had seen the silhouette, heard the engine, seconds before it -and just in time. Only just!

The Spad almost roared as it banked away. In the cockpit the Mexican, now one of Trys´ few officers, cackled gleefully. He was singing a song of dubious virtue in his most celebratory voice. Futile gunfire came from the Military Governor´s men below. Almost every window in the building-like jewels in a land of glassless homes-was gone, shot out. A few dead were now scattered around too, amongst the crystal shards of glass.

There was a polite knock at the door.

"WHAT?!"screamed the Military Governor.

A figure strolled casually in.

"You!"

"I am filled with joy to see you too, Governor, dear . A message from Colonel Fitzroy and Admiral Guiterrez for you: let us pass in peace and you will go unharmed. Hinder us and pay the price."

Stubbington fought hard and got himself under control.

"You will ,of course, be aware that I cannot comply ,Countess, not without a direct order to that effect from London or Delhi."

"Oh dear ,dear ,what a pity...how sad....and hmm, well, never mind."

"To the last man, my Lady. I hope your Admiral enjoys that arithmetic."

"*Sea!*" Avçi replied in her best Spanish, with a polite inclination of her head worthy of a court ambassador.

"So may it be. So be it,"she clarified-and with that she turned to leave.

Halfway to the door she paused and looked back.

"Oh....one more thing, Your ...ah...Excellency....nobody appears to have seen Kitty for a day or two. You really

should learn to take better care of that girl. Good day, sir!
"

....
....

"They tell me that there is no officer in the Empire handier with a pistol, Kitchener-Crane. Is that true? "

The young lieutenant made surprised but pleased noises, unsure for the moment of a worthy response.

"Well, you come highly recommended all round, man," the fellow continued ,not waiting for the response, "and - as such -we have something for you. We hope you can take care of it. "

Kitchener Crane listened for the next two minutes, appalled at times, frankly amazed at others but mostly feeling an odd mixture of fear and of being over-flattered. No matter. He had a job to do, it seemed. Duty called again. Even as he had been blissfully on his way back to Europe's welcoming embrace, said his wistful afterthought.

"Remind me who you were again, please, sir?"

"You may call me Thomson. I work for his Majesty at the Embassy. That´s all you need to know for now."

Oh .Oh bloody hell. Still ,duty.... The inner strength of character and force of will ,a hidden steeliness that had seen him salvage the situation at the fort, answered the call once more.

"Well, I accept the task. I am here to serve my country as best I might."

"Excellent! Fitch will give you the rest. A good day to you, *Captain* Kitchener- Crane."

....

Trys and Guiterrez were bidding each other farewell. A couple of empty bottles of very good wine were on the table. The communiqué from the Admiral´s people lay to one side.

"This puts us on opposing sides once again, hermano . A pity."

"As long as we agree that the other two are...."

"Expendable? Yes. Always agreed. It may be in their blood ,yes but we have spent years sharpening our knowledge to bear it like a sword...anyway , enough poetic nonsense, "said the Admiral with a grin.

"Till next time or Elysium, Trys."

"Till next time or the realms beyond the Styx, sir."

"So much for enough poetic nonsense, eh? "

With that they at least both parted quietly laughing ,as they bowed and went their separate ways.

…………………………………………………………………..

Abs Thorpe was whistling a merry tune to himself. Occasional words came forth to punctuate the gaps.

"….aloft a tree…..paint……walks with me….."

The Russian rifle had changed, transformed from something scrounged into a gleaming thing of deadly efficiency. It was polished ,cleaned and its sights now trimmed to near perfection. The slight hysterical air had gone from Thorpe altogether now. This was a fellow with a purpose ,a goal, after all. One of a possible two,he reminded himself. He just needed to consider which of the two goal ends the was going to take a run at. It was looking like the colonel would receive his vengeance. Abs was not fully party to Avçi´s deal with Arden. Not that it would have mattered….

 He was coming to have a grudging respect for the Countess ,or whoever the hell she actually was, though. Oh, she was undeniably charming and attractive and stirred the blood, all that lark but…well, he had no plans to wake up dead after a tryst with her, thanks anyway. It wasn´t so much even this fact, however. Like him, she was out here ,to all intents and purposes, alone. Despite this, she showed real guts. She never gave in. Never surrendered. THAT sat very well with Thorpe, every time.

……………………………………………………

Santísima madre! Avçi had not been making one of her tasteless jokes. It was not another lie. In the past, all of them had been pranks at his expense, essentially. To make the charming Raul look a fool. This time, however, she had actually spoken the truth.

He watched the aeroplane gain height and saw that he was, indeed, unharmed. The Mexican would keep his silence. He loved the thrill of flight and his favourite toy too much not to. He would not risk it being taken away. Good. That served their purpose.

…………………………………………………..

She was keeping this one. Well, it made life more of a challenge, brought complications .True. It left a vulnerability too…a way she could be got at. Also a fact. She would need time to think , to plan. She had spent years developing great self-control and self-discipline . Her other skills in her chosen trade too. It needed careful handling, considering that line of work. Yes, she realised she had been ambushed, unexpectedly , by unlooked-for feelings and by their strength. No matter. Even as her lip had began to curl into a sneer of disdain for her own weakness , however ,she had actually stopped herself . No matter. She despised any kind of cowardice, including that she'd seen others show in their amorous affairs. This just needed a different kind of fearlessness-and at showing that she was a master. She would face this down and deal with it, even as it lit something deep within her - and she planned to let that same flame take hold. Besides, she had her life's work of tipping the balance against unworthy men to be done...why should such men have all the fun, given that....and what better way to be remembered once departed than by one close to you who saw you favourably? What better way to found your legend?

As her breathing slowed and she stayed aglow, Avçi decided that yes, definitely, she was keeping this one. Oh, not solely for the delightful sensations only just fading from her body now, in this moment, nice though they were. Nor for any of a number of other shared intimate moments between them that had given rise to such feelings. Not even for the bonds and feelings of attachment in which weaker women let sex itself trap them, to her mind. No.

It was more that ...well, this one, once she had had the chance to get away from her stifling ,stuffy surroundings and be herself had shown herself to be clever but humble ,incredibly sweet and funny , and in her own way as charming as Avçi herself . Also... surprisingly capable ...but capable of understanding *her* too. Why she, Avçi, enjoyed doing such a dirty job so much. Another kind of soul, sure- but one who spoke to her very own. She had found someone who could easily grow to be her equal, if lent that chance. Someone who liked who she was , perhaps ,or, if not that ,at least understood what she was and why she was that way . She threw a leg across her lover, claiming her. Kitty murmured happily as Avçi kissed her again.

....

It was a sound at the edge of hearing but enough to have him awake. Osman had clawed his way up from the streets .He had not left the ability to be awake and alert instantly in his former hiding places there. He put the electric light right on.

Two shapes in ,lying still in the corner, looked like his minders . Someone was staring down a Webley revolver at him, however. That was more pressing. The face was handsome, features calm- but focused. The gun was not wavering ,not even slightly. That was unmissable.

"With His Majesty´s compliments, Mr Osman," Kitchener-Crane told him, on an uncharacteristic whim, then pulled the trigger.

....

Guiterrez settled himself at the edge of the field of opium poppies, a field glowing softly in the early sun. A chair had been set out for him. He took a few moments then began to regulate his breathing. Words older than Christendom sprang, like fire, into life in his mind, incantations passed down in an unbroken line of learning for centuries. Raising one arm, he stretched the other out to describe an arc and then a circle around himself.

He crouched briefly and let his fingers spend some moments touching the ground , almost like a caress, before standing again. Then ,finally, the fire of the words in his thoughts came forth into spoken words. The mere world of men was forgotten to him right now.

A small susurration of breeze stirred out in the field, turning some flowers and stems as it did so and began to grow itself,to take on strength and force. The breeze grew to be a wind,then a howling thing,as plants began to be uprooted.

"Uh...chief....you need to see this..."said young Armandad, from a curtained doorway in the village a little way off.

Words of an entirely different kind coloured the air as Anushirivan looked upon a static typhoon taking to life in the middle of his poppy plantation, felt the draught of the air being sucked past him towards it. A few moments later the whole thing began moving steadily towards the village.

Well, that should put Trys´ little metal gnat out of the picture too, mused Guiterrez.

....

The last messenger from their current employers brought interesting news. Also quite a bit more money than expected. They were no longer required but mission accomplished, thank you, as enough of the desired kind of trade was already rumbling down the old routes . If they had time they were welcome to enjoy their time where they were. Pleasure doing business with...and so the obsequious screed ran on. It had been Osman´s last composition, sent by the latest means of communication to Karachi by his associates and brought by rider from there.

Trys looked out across the camp. The men lacked a little in terms of presentation and turnout,:some unshaven faces, the odd ragged sleeve or strange set of boots- but with turnout their raggedness ended. He was happy to let that go out here in the field anyhow. They were soldiers of fortune, not the Household Cavalry. They had forged themselves and been forged, too, into a fine fighting unit. A ghost of an officer´s pride in his men from his Army days let a brief, fierce feeling of pride flare within him .Then it was gone. This was business, albeit a dirty one.

In less than half an hour he must lead them into one last battle under his command-and the head of the Conclave himself would be waiting for them.

o0o

The dude had become my best mate through us surviving this hell together. Lobo Sabadura was a fascinating mix . Half European aristocratic snob , half cosmopolitan party animal. My own corresponding characteristics sometimes emerged at exactly the right time to match these two of his. We were walking back to that pile of red bricks, our mansion-like prison, from a beach walk when Lobo, typically, spotted a girl.

" Whoooo is that ? "

Making matters worse he called out:

"Please give me a little of your time, for my world and my clock stopped when I set eyes on you, beautiful girl…"

"Oh, really? Well, mine didn´t …so do fuck off!" she told him.

I laughed so hard I nearly needed medical assistance. Lobo took it all in his stride with a smile and a shrug -and then a grin.

o0o

This was the Avçi swathed in her assassins´ black, no longer playing the aristo, all action first words second, all business. This Avçi made a sound, halfway between a laugh and a snarl, then stuck the adjutant, through the hand, with his pen, pinning the hand. He went to his drawer with the remaining hand-

"This, was it?" she asked quite calmly.

He had been watching her, through the other corner of his eye. He caught the gleam and heard a click. He saw she had his 1911. The bitch! She was tutting at him and his expression.

"It´s all right, my big brave boy, I need you alive. For now. Please give His Majesty´s British Embassy a message. For their colleagues in Istanbul. It reads : I don´t like competition. I expect to be hired myself next time. Kissses. Avçi Guzman. "

She paused. Looked down briefly.

"Guess it really is mightier than the sword."

She patted his face. Dismantling the Colt and dropping into her knapsack, she left before he could recover his thoughts or his dignity.

....

"You BETTER keep your end ,my brother…..I just stuck a damned flag in the map saying "Here we are!" to the British Empire! You better! You hear me?"

Avçi was almost incandescent with fury. Arden was calm incarnate.

"I will. Spaniards value our word and the truth….sister, dearest."

Her smile was icy enough to take the heat from the surrounding air, contrasting eerily with the ire in her voice.

"And our mother was the same woman…and if she believed in a person or a thing, she would have died for it," she hissed, eyes ablaze.

"I will keep my word. I will not intercede between you and Trys. That is ALL , though, no more."

She calmed a little. She could not, would not, let him undo all her hard work with his so-called scruples. She had come too far. She now also had another prize to keep. Could not? Better, she WOULD not let him. There was to be no failure on anyone's part. She , her brother and her lover would triumph-or face annihilation in trying.

"One thing Avçi….since that´s what you call yourself these days…."

"Ah. Now comes the best line of the night, I´m sure."

"It did work, your little test but….sorry, my sister….I still believe in HIM. The Lord. El Señor. Good rewards those who try, at least, to do it. This much I know for sure. "

" Don´t give a fig, frankly, Raul. You´re a fool but well, your life and your bloody funeral, eh? . ¡Suerte!"

Suddenly she was the sullen girl of fourteen once again, the daughter of some wealthy Turkish character he despised, stood on the dockside as their mother proudly bade him farewell on yet another voyage, the girl whose eyes silently ,fiercely but unmistakably disapproved of his leaving their mother- and of his doing so yet again-and possibly of his very existence. Meanwhile , their mother stubbornly refused to let her tears show as more than an added light in her eyes, held them back, he knew, till he had gone and the dock was empty of folk. On his return, Avçi had been gone.

Oh you do give a fig, all right, you do care, my sister…he thought to himself. Just not for the reasons and the motives I do. At which moment inspiration struck and he went to catch up with Trys and the rest.

……………………………………………………………………………….

113

"So you suggest we ….?"

"At least wear the trappings of revolutionaries, sir. It might just work. We might just make it out ,even now."

"Christ, Raul, no wonder they gave you a boat to command…that's a thing of evil genius," said Trys in awe, "Let's do it!"

"We generally prefer *ship* in English,Trys. Then ….viva la revolución, Colonel! Long live the revolution ,sir! "

"Aye ,aye, Captain! Up the revolution! "

Trys paused.

"Better explain to my quack it's just a brilliant disguise though. "

Raul Arden sobered rapidly.

"Indeed, yes. That we must."

………………………………………………………………………………………..

Avçi stopped at the summit of the hill overlooking the valley, centring her thoughts and calming her breathing first. Below her, Guiterrez's tornado had already wrought its destruction on the opium poppies, he village and since dissipated. Looking down once she had settle herself, Avçi spoke three simple lines.

"Not all perished in the flood, my Lords and fathers. I am of your line, look within me and see one of your own. I claim without fear, without rancour, the power that is mine!!"

She then raised her eyes to the heavens and let the moonlight shine on her as something began to surge through her. It was all she could do not to laugh aloud in wicked delight as she felt it flow into her being, completing it, completing her sense of who she was. She uttered a war cry instead and leaping, punched the air.

Elsewhere, Thorpe was calmly etching angular characters into a silver bullet. To him, these strange letters and their associated customs were nothing fantastical or magical, just something taught to him by the old girl who sometimes fed him or gave him work for a few pennies back in Yorkshire. They were part of life, the everyday. He glanced out of his little cave and saw two carrion birds. Smiling, he continued carving.

……………………………………………………………………………….

Trys had not the faintest idea what Guiterrez had in mind here. He was alone ,which meant that he intended to use his Arts rather than simple brute force but...well, his ignorance of the Spaniard´s plan was making Trys sufficiently uneasy that he had felt the need to have the whole band with him. Him AND his army. Overhead, the

115

Spad now soared once again too, an eerie sight underneath the moonlight.

Avçi was stepping onto the wind- ravaged poppy plantation, just at the edge of the foothills opposite, at the same moment. Guiterrez was lost in the words of an incantation literally plucked from the flames by an ancestor. Whilst two senior clerics of the Church had been busily arguing ,one bemoaning the loss of centuries of knowledge ,this one ancestor, a mere street urchin, had run in and hastily stuffed several volumes into a sack, then run off.

She had survived to marry a prominent nobleman . How she had managed THAT one remained shrouded in the mists of time -but manage it she had. His concentration was total in that instant ,as he focused on the words in old Arabic. He had heard the flying pest buzzing and the rumble of the waggons and trucks of Trys´ band but he no longer minded them. He was one with the magic now. This was do or die and if he died within his magic, he died well.

Then something DID trouble him. A power perhaps equally as ancient as the sages of the Nile -and it was growing close. In fact, he heard the slightest sound behind him, as though there were soft footsteps in the very field itself.

Then a finger tapped his shoulder. Well, he, the Master , though humble ,as his calling demanded , was also wise.

He was not about to fall for this old trick from ANY quarter. As a voice uttered the word it once used in practice drills , ones where live bullets would have killed, however, a voice of one he had once trained to kill…..those same ancient words began to fail him in his shock:

" Pum ! " Avçi told him.

Suddenly furious, he turned, turned to face her….

…………………………………………………………………………………………………

………………………………………………………

Thorpe calmly waited where he now was, perched on a boulder ,out in the same field. He waited until the first soldiers came into sight, waited until their commanding officer did too, leading –as so often- from the front. He let them come close and heeded the old military injunction to wait until he could see the whites of their eyes, before breaking cover from the mangled vegetation.

He blocked Trys´ path, cocked the Russian rifle and said : "Halt!"

o0o

I was walking down that same narrow corridor, the one I had been rushed down on arrival, on admission. Today, though, sunlight pouring in through the old sash windows of the onetime manor house mansion was painting paler patches on the hospital greens and cheap but durable institutional carpet. It was discharge day...I was going home!

"Waiiiiiituppppp!!! Wait up, will ya?"

Lobo was hurtling down the sunlit corridor, past the old brass-handled doors.

o0o

Guiterrez, who had wheeled sharply to confront Avçi ,caught sight of something ageless and profoundly evil in her eyes -and promptly wished he had run instead. She noticed this in his change of expression.

"It may be....a little late....Admiral...but...I´d like to give the great Torquemada a present. Yes, yes, that would be nice, I think. Fitting . Compliments of my forefathers..." she told him.

The Admiral went up like a lighted torch and caught the poppy field aflame as he did so. The fire and heat were so bright, so intense, that he barely had time to scream before he was consumed, becoming just the spark to light the opium crop into its own inferno .

Raul was here too, somewhere. That complicated matters. He had made his allegiance clear. She was working on a simpler arithmetic though : her, Kitty and MAYBE Raul . He, too, could go if he got in her way, though.

Trys saw his teacher, his respected adversary at other times, go up like bonfire night and from his sudden sadness at this sight an ire like none he had ever known was brought to life. Words of power flew from his lips as his men fought those of the local warlords and some cutthroats hired by Guiterrez.

The field became a howling firestorm and the few surviving soldiers had soon either fled or perished. Somewhere a part of him was further saddened at this loss but, right here, right now and like the Admiral mere minutes before, he was lost within his magic.

All around, there was searing heat and flame. Through it, her hair swirling as though she swam beneath a fiery ocean, Avçi walked towards him. His Art kept him intact-for now. Arden was walking alongside him and then, there was a soft blue glow within the fiery field and the Captain was gone. This seemed to scare his sister-but very ,very ,briefly. A second later ,her usual composure had returned.

They continued towards each other. As they finally stood a metre apart, Trys spoke:

"I see what you have become. I will not be cowed by it, though. Look at me and see why I have done what I have done...and know this: you cannot defeat that which drove me. It is what makes men men , not beasts."

" *Really, Colonel?* If it wasn´t for my kind you would never have had the inspiration...."

Avçi sighed. It was a sigh of frustration and anger. She continued. Her last few words were pure derision.

"I´ve come into my own, love. I´m here to stay. You win...for today. Don´t get used to it, though, soldier blue."

It was as though black-feathered wings actually sprouted from her as she began to levitate before his very eyes and leave the field of battle. She was at least consistent: he had always thought her an evil bitch from Raul´s few stories about her and his own limited experience-and this was true to form. Oh well...

Trys let himself calm down and let the fires subside further before turning to leave too , albeit on foot.

Thorpe calmly waited. He was perched on a boulder ,out in the same field. As he saw the Colonel come into view, he hopped down. He blocked Trys´ path, cocked the Russian rifle and said : "Halt!"

Thorpe took in the officer's improvised revolutionary uniform but wasn't taken in himself.

"A little late to the party, aren't we, Sergeant? " asked Trys, whilst calmly approaching, affecting an unruffled air as he did so.

"Perhaps . Be that as it may, I can't let you leave here, sir. It changes history. Changes it too much. Not good, that. A few ripples in the millpond are one thing, slinging in a boulder….? Nah. Weird and not in a good way. Not going to happen."

It was the matter-of-fact tone , the one that stated this is what will be, that drew Trys up short, rather than the simple suicidal bravery of the man in front of him. In that awful moment his blood ran cold. His time had come. He could sense as much.

"Ever heard of a place called Folkvang , Colonel Fitzroy? See you there if you're worthy.Oh and…. can you tell yer 792 from yer 303?"

With which words he shot his former CO dead.

………………………………………………………………………………………

A highway on the shore of the Emerald Isle wound away before him. The sun was out and there was an old sailing vessel out in the bay, anchored upon the sparkling seas. A hand held his, a smiling face looked up at him as he smiled upon seeing her own. He was with his girl once more.

"Faith hope and love….of these the greatest is love…welcome home," said a voice that filled his being.

The light upon the waves grew brighter but not blinding, as did the sun in the sky and the light in his lover's eyes. An unexpected sense of peace and contentment filled that same being. He was home. He remembered nothing else now and nothing else mattered.

……………………………………………………………………………………………..

"Mother…."said Arden.

The figure held a hand out towards him. She laughed softly, delightedly, as he spoke. She was lit from behind by a light that was powerfully bright yet somehow did not hurt his sight.

"In a manner of speaking, perhaps, Captain Raul Arden Of His Majesty's Spanish Armada. In a manner of speaking…well, you must go back, shortly, I'm afraid….and you must forget you were ever here. Take my hand, Captain."

He had a feeling arguing was even more pointless than usual here. He did as asked. The light shifted, did things that baffled him. She was…quite the most beautiful thing he had ever seen and not in the way any of his supposed conquests had been. Despite her kindness and her use of his rank, he felt very small indeed…

……………………………………………………………………………………………
…..

Avçi dropped softly back to earth to find Thorpe watching her with mild interest. She scrutinised him closely. He took in her assassin´s garb.

"I preferred the frock and parasol but…to each his-or her-own ,I suppose. And the wedding´s off now, anyway."

Despite herself and the ageless power she now felt coursing through her, she burst out laughing.

"Oh don´t worry, Abstinence Thorpe, I was never a nice girl anyway and isn´t that what every mother wants…?"

"Blowed if I know, your ladyshipness. Mine never introduced herself."

Damn him! She was off again. Then ,as her last few chuckles died down, she peered more closely. Ah. This one would be okay.

"Hmmm .I see now you have your own secrets, Sergeant. Fair play. It has been a pleasure," and she extended her hand.

He took it, afraid that he might appear rude and spoil the farewell .He proceeded to unsling his rifle. He emptied the magazine and checked the chamber before passing it across to her, the bolt open.

"Been using this one 'cause leaving a signature is never good. It can be followed, like a calling card. They tell me you like the things though. Tek it. I'm done here anyway."

o0o

Lobo put his hands on his knees to recover from the sprint.

"Thanks for the pendant thing...the charm. Bit gay, but thanks anyway."

"No worries. You out soon?"

"Next week, they reckon."

"Well, if it's Tuesday, I guess I'll see you..."

"Yeah, yeah, just make sure you don't come back HERE yourself, ok?"

Miss So-do-fuck-off was walking up the same corridor in a leisurely fashion, just a handbag slung over one shoulder to give any clue she was out today too. As she looked us over, she took in my bags.

"Hello. Want a lift? As a one-off, that is."

"You have a car? This changes EVERYTHING, "said Lobo.

"Sure does. I get to get away from you."

She turned to me and held out a hand for one of the bags, then shrugged and continued walking when I hesitated. I made a 'phone gesture to Lobo, hugged him briefly and with that, called out that a lift would be welcome, thanks and walked out into the morning air.

oOo

Arden opened his eyes to find himself on deck, a glass of wine in his hand. A coffin was secured to the deck. Someone had painted a single peace lily on the lid. His friend knew peace too now, he felt sure. Maguire was telling some anecdote or other of his own as some of the few survivors listened attentively. He felt eyes upon him and looked across towards the bow end. His sister, once again playing the noblewoman, was chatting to her companion whilst watching him. She inclined her head in that courtly gesture she had mastered so well. He laughed softly. Even though she was horrible, well, some might say evil, she was his sister. He returned the gesture. He had had a pleasant doze, it seemed, and woken to another mariner's tale from Maguire. He cleared his throat:

"Gentlemen, let me tell you about the time I met the duke's daughter..."

125

Mark Maguire groaned and went to fetch more wine for them all. The Mexican smiled and held his counsel. The poor doctor hadn´t heard this one –yet. The sea was calm enough to be pleasant, choppy enough for there to be wind to fill the sails. A skilled seafarer, he could smell the sea and feel its swell beneath them. He was sailing across his second home towards his own.

oOo

I threw my things on the backseat and shut the passenger door firmly. We were leaving....back to life and to the here and now. I introduced myself, as I hadn´t yet, really. She did too. I apologised for Lobo.

"Oh , I´m used to it. I expect he likes the thrill of the chase,or something else prehistoric. I´m more of a Friday night´s for vandalism and screwing on the floor sort of girl, I´m afraid."

I laughed. She then saw my bundle of mismatched handwritten, typed and pencil-scrawled pages, all bound up in a folder on my lap.

"Writer, are you?"

I nodded. She smiled for the first time and it was like the whole interior lit up. I shook myself. Nope, not that strain all over again. Not yet, anyway. She appeared to notice somehow and –unfazed and unruffled-turned her dark eyes back to her driving. We were going home. I had made it through. Thank the stars for that!

"Well, anyway," she added "I must say that that DOES sound exciting…"

[THE END/FIN]

.